A JINGLE VALLEY ~~WEDDING~~

New York executive Julie Tate knows what it takes to win in the financial world, but her big-city success could never prepare her for her latest career move. When her brother abandons the failing family farm, Julie hopes its salvation lies in transforming it into western Massachusetts's newest premier wedding venue. With her social-savvy friend Freddy in her corner, Julie feels infallible.

But as their bank account dwindles and one obstacle after another crops up, the business partners wonder if their venture is doomed for failure before the first bride walks down the aisle. Maybe the best way to succeed in a business based on romance is to find one.

Also by **MARTHA REYNOLDS**

Chocolate for Breakfast

Chocolate Fondue

Bittersweet Chocolate

Bits of Broken Glass

Best Seller

A JINGLE VALLEY ~~WEDDING~~

ISBN-13: 978-1518707575

ISBN-10: 1518707572

THOMAS

Thomas called Julie when he knew she wouldn't be home. *Coward.* He could have dialed her cell number, or her office number, but at two o'clock on a snowy Wednesday afternoon, he pushed the buttons to connect with her home answering machine. He waited for the beep, then began speaking, reciting lines from a script he'd prepared in advance.

"Jules, it's Tommy. Listen, I hate to do this over the phone, but I'm done. I can't do it for one more day. I'm heading to Arizona to visit Don and Linda. One of the guys will take care of everything while I'm gone, but Jules, I don't know when I'll be back."

He disconnected the call, knowing he'd been abrupt, knowing she'd freak out when she listened, which might not be until later that night. He printed out the address and phone number in Tucson and left it on the dining room table, then took one last walk through the big house where he'd grown up.

"Sorry, Mom and Dad," he whispered to the walls. "I tried, I really did. Maybe Julie can make this work, but I can't."

As a mustard-yellow taxi turned into the long gravel drive that led to the old farmhouse, Thomas pulled the heavy oak door behind him and turned the key in the lock, then bent and tucked the key under a rock with a splotch of white paint on it. He picked up his bags and walked to the approaching cab.

JULIE

She needed coffee. That experiment where she tried to rid herself of caffeine and sugar lasted for exactly two days, and was a bad idea to begin with. Julie had an assistant who was more than willing to fetch a nonfat latte and chocolate chip cookie from the place next door, but she craved a break from fluorescent and blue light.

"Harmony, I'll be back in ten minutes. Cover my phone, will you, please?" Julie passed by her assistant's desk and paused. "Can I get you anything?"

"I'll go for you. You don't have to," the young woman said. Harmony pushed her chair back and started to stand, but Julie raised her hand, palm out. Stop. Like The Supremes did in that song.

"I could use some fresh air," she explained with a smile. "You want one of those cream cheese brownies?" She knew Harmony's weakness.

"Oh, man, those things! Sooo good," Harmony moaned. "No more after New Year's," she muttered, and Julie didn't believe a word of it.

"Try to hang on. I'll be back in ten."

"Take your coat, it's freezing out!" Harmony called to her boss's retreating back.

Julie ignored her, but regretted that choice as soon as she stepped outside. The wind blew around the edge of the tall building and cut into her like a hundred frozen knives. She hurried to the recently-opened coffee shop two doors down and pulled the door closed behind her. The place was empty, and she imagined everyone else had been smart enough to pick up their coffee on the way in to work. A man with curly black hair and sexy stubble looked up from behind the counter.

"You should have worn a coat," he said, flashing perfect, shiny teeth. Those had to be fake, Julie thought.

"I know," she said, rubbing her upper arms. It was toasty inside the little coffee shop. And it smelled good, like sinful carbs.

"You need something hot," he said. "Chocolate? Coffee?"

He was hot, but Julie figured that wasn't what he meant. "Nonfat latte, a chocolate chip cookie, and one of those cream cheese brownies," she said, pointing to a marbled confection behind a glass display case. It was as big as her hand. Did Harmony want coffee?

"And a small coffee, too. Cream and sugar."

"I'm Axel, by the way. Don't recall seeing you in here before, but you must work close by if you're out without your coat." Julie watched as his waxed-paper-covered hand grasped the bigger of the two cream cheese brownies. He took a new piece of paper and picked up a giant cookie, then placed both pieces in a pale blue bakery box. He turned his back to her to make the latte.

Julie stared, mesmerized, from the other side of the great glass barrier. Broad shoulders strained a snug black t-shirt. She lifted up on her toes to peek over the counter. Slim waist and a very nice butt in jeans. A white waist apron covered him in front, which was just as well, since (a) she wasn't looking, and (b) she had to get back to work. And why hadn't Harmony mentioned him before?

Axel. She guessed he was born in the eighties, and that his parents were big fans of Guns N' Roses. Maybe they even left out the 'e' in his name. That would make him between twenty-five and thirty. Not too young. Right?

"Miss?" His voice was as creamy as vanilla icing. Julie swayed slightly before blinking hard.

"What?"

"You were somewhere else. Twelve-fifty." He grabbed his upper lip with his bottom teeth, and she wanted to kiss him. For a really long time. She wanted his stubble to rough up her skin, and leave telltale redness on her cheeks and neck. Instead, she dug in her purse and pulled out a twenty. He rang up the sale and handed her a few bills and two quarters. Julie glanced around for a tip jar but seeing none, put the money back in her purse.

"Hope to see you again." His eyes were nearly black and fringed with impossibly long lashes. He was almost too pretty, Julie thought. Axel placed the bakery box and two cups of coffee on the counter, then reached underneath for one of those cardboard cup holders and wedged the cups into it, at opposite corners.

Julie inhaled deeply, needing oxygen, and needing to be outside in the cold air. She made a mental promise never to let Harmony do the coffee run again.

"I'll see you tomorrow," she said, and it came out all breathy. She really didn't want to leave.

"Julie?"

She turned at the sound of a painfully familiar voice.

"Christopher!" She looked up into the face of the man who was, and then wasn't, The One. God, he looked good. Dumping her three years ago certainly hadn't aged him, not one stupid day. What was he doing around here, anyway?

As if he'd read her mind, he said, "I started a new job about a month ago. You still with PCM?" Julie nodded dumbly.

Her secret wish that Christopher was fat and bald hadn't come true. He told her he was a junior partner in the white-shoe, old-money law firm of Applewhite, Skipworth, and Doddridge. He didn't call it white-shoe or old-money. But that's what AS&D was. And Christopher fit right in.

"That's wonderful!" she said, clenching her teeth before giving him a wide smile. Maybe he would remember her fake smile when he saw it. She held the pastry box in one hand, the cardboard tray in the other hand, and she wondered how long she'd have to make inane small talk with her ex-boyfriend.

"And, I'm a daddy now. Twins! A boy and a girl, three months ago." He pulled out his phone to show her a photo. Julie forced herself to gush at the perfect little replicas of Christopher and his beautiful, former underwear model wife whose first name she couldn't recall. It was a color. Teal? No. Burnt Sienna? Hmm. Cerise! Yes, of course, Cerise. Perfect, leggy, size zero Cerise. Even after having twins.

She shifted her weight and Christopher swiftly moved to open the door.

"Do you think you can make it okay?"

"I do," she said, instantly regretting it. Why couldn't she have simply said yes?

***

After dropping Harmony's coffee and brownie on her desk, Julie closed the door to her office and slipped off her shoes. She wrapped her hands around the cardboard cup of hot coffee and felt the warmth spread through her icy fingers. Seeing Christopher was a jolt. They'd been together for two years and four months. Enough time together that she felt sure about him. Enough time together that their arguments seemed only to strengthen their relationship. But then, a few weeks before everything ended, they'd had a serious talk about children. They were both in their early thirties, and Christopher had asked. How ready was she to start a family? Julie had answered honestly, of course. Kids weren't on her horizon, and might never be. She couldn't commit to a timeline. A woman at thirty-one had to at least have a timeline, according to Christopher. Three weeks later, he'd brought flowers and ended it. Ended them. She remembered his words – "we're at different places and I know where I need to be headed." Well, at least he didn't use a sports metaphor to break up with her.

Since then, Julie had had maybe a dozen dates, ten of them duds. At thirty-four, she could say she was surer of what she wanted, but uncertain as to whether she'd ever get it. Christopher was married and a father, with a well-paying job and a house in Connecticut. And he still had time on his side. Julie had devoted so much time to work, and to getting ahead, that she felt she may have missed her chance. How ridiculous was that? Thirty-four is not old, she tapped out on her desk with her nails. And yet it was.

Her four closest girlfriends were all married. Sure, they still had the occasional girls' night out, and when Lauren and Jake hosted their every-other-month dinner parties, they always dredged up a single guy for Julie if Julie didn't have a date. But none of those men was ever a match. And she knew she probably wasn't what they were looking for, either. These were guys who wanted what her friends all had: stability, a baby or two, a house in Westchester or Darien. Julie never gave any indication that she wanted that. Marriage? Yes. Children? Yes, she would admit now that she felt a vague longing for a child, even though it created a ticking clock in her head that was disquieting. When she pondered her future, ten years ahead, she couldn't see herself living in a three-bedroom Cape with a gas grill on the back patio. With a couple of babies, sixteen months apart (because she didn't have time on her side), an endless stream of disposable diapers and pacifiers. A husband who took the train into the city and came home after six, expecting dinner. She wasn't Betty Draper, the early version. But her girlfriends seemed to revel in that life, and whenever they gathered, they all shared stories with the same themes: Blair has a tooth! Colby finally used the potty on his own! You have to try this recipe! Julie had nothing to offer but her fake smile and feigned interest in Apple Cider Baked Chicken.

At the same time, she didn't know how long she'd stay in the city. Manhattan, vibrant with the surge of human passions, could age a girl. The little bistro she'd called her second home for the past six years was now filled with patrons ten years younger than she was. Everyone was younger, it seemed.

Her cell phone vibrated on her desk. Ah, Freddy. Her only male friend, really her best friend, had just ended a year-long relationship and they often compared notes on the dismal dating scene around them.

"Doll! How's your day going?" he asked in a rusty, just-woken-up voice.

"Fine, I guess. Half the office seems to be on vacation already."

"I still need to buy something for my sister's kid. Come with me after work; I don't know how to shop for a twelve-year-old girl."

Julie laughed. "You always put it off until the last minute."

"Wrong! Christmas is days away. Pick you up at six?"

"Make it five-thirty. And can we eat first?" She looked down at her cookie, with one big bite missing. She was having lunch with the boss, and he'd mentioned that new Tex-Mex place. She wrapped the cookie in a napkin and tossed it in the wastepaper basket. She'd have a salad with Maxwell and eat dinner with Freddy. Counterbalance.

"See you then," Freddy said before hanging up.

***

Maxwell escorted Julie into Mariachi Blues. "They have an amazing tortilla pie," he said, and her skirt instantly felt tighter.

"I'm having an early dinner with a friend, so I think a salad would work for me." Julie didn't run every morning like her boss, who, at fifty-two, recently appeared on the cover of New York Men's Health magazine. She assumed that a fitness nut such as Maxwell would also care about what he ate, but he grabbed a couple of hot dogs from Omar's sidewalk cart twice a week.

"I wanted to spend some time with you before I head out on vacation," he said, pausing as a waiter rattled off the daily special. After they'd given their orders, he resumed.

"We'll be at the Aspen house, but you have all the numbers. Cell service can be spotty at times, especially if the weather's bad. And Barton's staying in the city," he added, referring to the managing partner of the firm, who was nearly eighty and should have been announcing his retirement.

"It's quiet in the office, and I imagine it'll be that way until after New Year's," Julie said, sipping unsweetened iced tea. "Only a few of the junior associates are sticking around, trying to drum up some new business."

Maxwell nodded, concentrating on the multi-layered rectangle on his plate. Julie noted corn, black beans, ground beef, and loads of melted cheese. She wished the restaurant was one of those places that gave you unlimited chips and salsa.

Maxwell wiped his mouth with an orange linen napkin. "There are lots of changes coming in the new year, Julie." He wouldn't look at her, and it dawned on her that he brought her to lunch to fire her. Oh God, she was about to be fired! She was gripped with a sense of suffocation and panic, and pushed her salad to the side. She had some money, she'd been a good saver, but why? She'd done a great job as Compliance Officer. It wasn't like this was her dream job, and she didn't want to do it for the rest of her life, but fire her now?

"You're a valuable member of PCM, Julie. We all appreciate you, but I'd be lost without you." He reached into his jacket and pulled out a small envelope. "Merry Christmas," he said.

Her hand was shaking as she accepted his gift. "Thank you," she whispered, the two little words catching in her dry throat. She wasn't part of the leadership team, but her position was important. She didn't open the envelope in his presence; instead, she slipped it into her purse. Julie knew it was a gift card to Crate & Barrel, one of the firm's clients. Everyone received similar gift cards last year, and the year before.

"Hey, let's get a couple of churros," Maxwell said, signaling the waiter.

***

Freddy and Julie navigated the sidewalks around Rockefeller Center. She had to hold his elbow so as not to be swept off the pavement by the tsunami of shoppers rushing by.

"Here, Freddy? Really? What are you, a tourist?"

He laughed and pulled her into Bloomingdale's. The crowds were worse inside, if that was even possible.

"Okay, okay, you're right," he said. "I'll get her a gift card."

"You could have done that online!"

"And miss seeing this expression on your face? Not a chance, girlfriend."

Julie let her shoulders sag and followed him to a cash register, where he bought a $250 gift card for a twelve-year-old girl.

"Rich uncle, indeed," she murmured.

"I have to spoil someone," Freddy said. "Come on, I'll buy you dinner." He grabbed her hand and led her through the throngs of people, most of them not even shopping. The out-of-towners just wanted to be inside a famous department store in Manhattan days before Christmas.

"Please God, not around here, I'm begging you. Take me to that little Indian place near the water thing." Even the sidewalk was too crowded.

He lowered his chiseled chin and looked down at her with half-closed eyes. "Oh, the place by the water thing."

"You know." She took his lapel and pulled him closer as a family of four squeezed behind her.

"The wonderful thing about it, dear, is that I *do* know what you mean. At least we won't have crowds - everyone around here wants to go to Serendipity for frozen hot chocolate." He raised his free arm to hail a taxi.

Freddy was model-handsome and Julie watched with amusement as middle-aged women stopped and stared. Tall and lean, he had wavy brown hair and piercing gray eyes. He used to work for one of the bigger construction firms in the city, then he got laid off in the recession, and he started doing renovation work on his own. While he was generous with his only niece, Julie knew that he lived carefully. He understood that work was sporadic.

During dinner, they commiserated about their miserable plans for Christmas.

"Come with me to Hoboken, then," Freddy said. "My sister's cool, and her husband has a big Italian family. It'll be fun for you."

Julie shook her head. "No, I'm taking the train to see Tommy on the farm." She gave Freddy a wicked grin. "Why don't *you* come with *me*?"

"All those cows! No, thanks. Besides, you don't really like it, either, city girl." He pulled apart a flat round naan and stuffed a piece in his mouth.

"But it's my home. The family home. It's full of memories. And Tommy's been having a hard time of it lately, I can tell. The last couple of conversations we've had, he seemed so down. I think it's the onset of winter that does it to him. I'll go and cheer him up."

"But you'll be back for New Year's Eve, right?"

"I'll be back," she said, patting his hand. "And I'll go with you to your party. Even if there won't be any straight guys there. But it's not like I have any other plans."

"Hey! There will so be. We don't exclude. Rob and Greg know tons of interesting people. And you have to come with me. Help me find someone to kiss when the clock strikes twelve."

She and Freddy had kissed once, soon after they'd met, when Julie was drunk. What she did remember of that kiss was very nice. That was right before he confessed to her that a woman's lips did nothing for him. She took the last piece of naan from the basket.

"Five days up at the farm with Tommy will do me in," she said with a laugh.

Two hours later, Julie was back in her apartment. She shrugged off her coat, kicked off her ankle boots, and put her little cardboard box of chicken tikka in the refrigerator. She stilled when she saw the blinking green light on her answering machine. No one ever called her at home anymore; everyone who mattered called her cell. She pushed a button to listen and heard Tommy's deep voice. Those last six words – "I don't want to come back" – gave her a shiver.

"What the hell, Tommy," Julie cried to the empty apartment. "What the hell."

THOMAS

Thomas arrived at Albany International Airport and paid the driver. It was an expensive ride, but he couldn't drive his truck and just leave it in long-term parking. His flight was in ninety minutes, so he walked up to the ticket counter and checked his bag.

"One way to Phoenix, sir?"

"Right."

After changing planes at Chicago's Midway, he was on his way to Phoenix, where his brother Don and Don's wife Linda had lived for the past twenty years. The only thing he'd told his older brother was that he was taking a much-needed vacation and looked forward to visiting with them over the holidays. Don probably figured Thomas had help for the farm, enough for two weeks. Or maybe Don didn't think about it at all. Ten years older than Thomas, Don was retired from the Air Force and he and Linda, empty nesters now, lived just outside Phoenix in a spacious home. While waiting for his connecting flight, Thomas used his phone to check the weather and his heart soared when he saw a row of five suns. Low seventies in December! There was already snow on the ground in Dalton, the result of some earlier than predicted winter weather last week. Don liked to play golf, and Thomas looked forward to a few days on the links.

Eric, the eldest of the Tate brothers, was flying in from Austin tomorrow. Thomas hadn't seen Eric for years, and he wondered how that reunion might go. Eric should have taken on the responsibilities of Jingle Valley when Dad got sick, but he'd already built up his business in Austin and couldn't leave Texas. Or wouldn't leave Texas. Don was still in the Air Force and drew a pass. Ella, second oldest, had settled in San Diego with a woman named Margot and had little contact with anyone. So the job fell to Thomas to keep the farm alive. He'd held a brooding resentment against his brothers, even as he easily acknowledged he had no reason to. A couple of bad decisions in his twenties had brought Thomas back home to live rent-free on the farm. His mother was nearly eighty at the time and could barely keep up with day to day living. Still, as soon as Thomas had dropped his belongings in his old bedroom at the top of the stairs, he was expected to start working. The cows and the chickens. The stalls, the coops. He was never meant to do farm work, but his divorce had wiped him out. That and an investment in penny stocks that went south in a hurry.

Both of his brothers had told him they wanted no stake in the farm. The land was worth plenty, and Thomas knew that he could sell it and move to the southwest, where he wouldn't have to put up with cold and snow anymore. After his mother died, Eric, Ella, and Don all signed off on paperwork that left Thomas and Julie co-owners of Jingle Valley Farm. But Julie would never sell, he was sure. This was the family home for generations and she'd fight him on this. She was the sentimental one in the family. He glanced at his watch. She'd probably be home by now, would have listened to his well-rehearsed message on her answering machine, and would be planning how to kill him.

He rubbed his temples. He loved his sister so much, and this was one of the hardest things he'd ever done, but he couldn't take it for another season. Living out in western Massachusetts was ageing him faster than it should have. At thirty-six, he was divorced with no kids. If he wanted to start a family, he'd better get moving. He and Tracy had married young, too young, and she'd pushed him about babies right from the start. He'd wanted to wait. After the economy tanked, he couldn't commit to children, not until he was back on his feet and could provide for his family. Tracy didn't want to wait. Six months after they'd split, she'd moved in with a guy up in Nashua. She probably had a few kids by now. Good for her, Thomas thought. Now it's my time.

Julie would probably stay single, he mused as he stared out the tiny airplane window at the kaleidoscope of greens and browns below. Even though she had the looks, she was so driven, so married to her job in New York, that he couldn't imagine her slowing down enough even to say 'I do.' Unless she married someone just like her, then they could go about their insane jobs at their frantic paces, stopping every few days to smile at each other as they raced out of their apartment on their way to work.

No, that wasn't what Thomas wanted. He enjoyed the pace of life at the farm, he liked the way folks lived more simply, but he needed warmth and sunshine more than three months a year. Hopefully Don would help him find a job out in Arizona.

***

Thomas stood in the great room of Don and Linda's house and was reminded of a massive wooden cathedral, not that he'd been inside a church for years. He'd want a house like this, once he settled down and got a job. Modern and spacious, not a hundred-year-old structure with a leak in the roof. The sprawling hacienda ranch had beamed ceilings and a guest house. There was a swimming pool in back, and even a jogging trail that wound its way into woods behind the property. Thomas wondered how much a place like this would cost, but figured he should wait a day or so before asking his brother.

"We set you up in the pool house, Tom," Linda said as she opened the back door and stepped onto a concrete patio. Thomas followed and squinted against the glare that was reflected on white patio furniture. Turquoise water in the pool sparkled. "Don and I fixed it up for houseguests; that way you have your privacy. I can't tell you how happy we are that you're staying with us!" Her lips loosened into a faint smile. "I'll leave you to get settled. Feel free to have a swim if you want." She turned back into the main house.

Thomas carried his bags into the guest house and flopped onto the bed. Man, all I'd need is a little place like this, he thought, not a massive house. A cottage. With a swimming pool. Maybe he could rent this little house from Don until he found a place of his own. He unzipped his bag and pulled out swim trunks. She said he could swim. The sun was warm on his bare back and he knew he'd burn, but asking Linda to rub sunscreen on his skin seemed a bit awkward. He wasn't sure she was all that pleased to have him visiting.

He walked to the shallow end and stepped in. It felt like a bath, and he pushed forward, breaststroking to the opposite end. Just in case Linda was watching from the kitchen window, Thomas swam ten laps without stopping, then hoisted himself up onto the pool's concrete lip. He shook the water from his hair and looked down at his ghostly white skin. A couple of weeks here and he'd turn brown, like everyone else.

Back in the pool house, he showered, combed his damp hair and dressed in clean khaki shorts and a white shirt. He knocked lightly on the back door before letting himself into the house.

"So, Tommy, how's it feel to not need a coat in December?" Linda asked. She stood at the counter, chopping peppers into a confetti of red and green and yellow. She scooped up the pieces with her hands and dropped them into a big glass bowl, then began chopping red onion.

"Pretty great," he said, lowering his frame onto a barstool. "I could get used to this so fast." He picked an olive from a white bowl on the counter and savored the salty tang of it.

"That's what everyone says when they come to Arizona," Linda said, so quietly Thomas almost didn't hear her. He saw her glance at the clock on the wall.

He heard the whirr of a motor and saw Linda's shoulders drop an inch. "Don's home," she said. She finished with the onion and turned to the sink to wash her hands.

***

Don held a bottle of wine in his hands. "Tommy? Malbec?" He took a corkscrew and deftly uncorked the bottle.

"I don't really drink wine much. Got any beer?"

"I'll join you." Linda pulled two bottles from the refrigerator and popped the tops. After slicing a lime into eighths, she pushed one into the top of each bottle and left them there, sticking out like chartreuse thumbs. "That's how we drink beer around here," she explained with a grin as she slid one bottle across the smooth granite.

Thomas pushed the lime in and had to cover the top with his thumb while the beer settled. Then he raised his bottle in salute and took a long drink. "So, Eric gets in tomorrow?"

Don nodded and settled on the barstool next to his younger brother. "We do supper pretty casual most evenings. We'll have a big dinner tomorrow night when Eric's here."

"Sure," said Thomas. Eric's arrival was a big deal. Eric was a big deal.

Linda placed a glass bowl on the counter. Besides the brightly-colored peppers and onion, it contained shredded chicken, corn, and black beans. And something small and green and leafy that Thomas guessed was cilantro. Linda spooned the mixture onto three plates. She reached behind her for a woven basket, laid a white cloth napkin inside, and pulled flat pitas from the oven with tongs.

"Dinner is served," she said as she sat. "Tommy, how's Julie? Is she staying in the city for the holidays?"

Thomas took another long swig before answering. "Yeah, I think that's what she said. She's always working, you know?" He had turned his phone off just before they started dinner, knowing Julie would call when she listened to the message he'd left. It was nine o'clock in New York. He wanted to check his phone but willed himself to leave it alone.

"Well, we would have loved for her to fly out with you. Don, when's the last time we saw Julie?"

Don shrugged and chewed on a piece of bread. Thomas watched Linda watch Don. When her dark eyes met his, Thomas saw an undefined sadness that enveloped her face. Something was going on between the two of them, and Thomas was the unwelcome guest. Maybe it was better that he was in the pool house. Maybe it would be better once Eric arrived.

JULIE

When Julie's call to Thomas went directly to voice mail, she seethed. Dammit, Tommy! He wouldn't even give her the decency of a conversation? Fine.

"Tommy, call me back. I'll give you a half hour to listen to this message and call me back; otherwise, I'm calling Don at the house. You cannot just leave the family farm. Listen, I know it's been rough for you lately, but we have to talk about this. It's you and me, right? So, just call me."

She disconnected the call and paced six steps before she hit a wall in her tiny apartment, so she pivoted and took six steps in the opposite direction. It was nearly eleven, and she should be in bed, but this situation had her so wired she might as well have had two cups of coffee with Freddy. It was nine o'clock in Phoenix. They wouldn't be in bed yet. Why did she say she'd give him a half hour? She watched the clock as she paced. After twenty minutes, she dialed the number for Don and Linda's landline and waited.

"Hello?" Linda's voice greeted her.

"Linda! Hi, it's Julie." She willed her voice to be calm and upbeat, even as her free hand drummed incessantly on her thigh.

"Julie! We were just talking about you. How are you, honey? Oh, we'd have loved it if you flew out with Tommy. Tommy? Come back, it's Julie! Oh, he just stepped outside. Well, never mind, you and I can catch up."

"I want to catch up with you, too! I just needed a quick word with Tommy, though."

"Oh! Well, hang on a second." Julie counted to herself and waited until Linda came back on the line. "Those boys, they were already halfway across the yard. I couldn't get him, hon. But let's you and me chat a bit and he'll be back. Don smokes one cigarette, after supper, every day. I let it go, you know? It's not the worst thing he could be doing." She heard Linda cough. "Now, how's everything in New York City?"

Julie could play Tommy's little game, she thought. "Everything's fine here, thanks. A lot colder than where you are, I'm sure." She'd keep Linda talking until they came back to the house.

"Well, we get a little chilly at night but the days have been glorious," Linda said with a chuckle. "Tommy says you're working too hard. I hope you're planning some time off for the holidays? Oh wait. Don, is that you?"

Julie waited but heard nothing on the other end. When Linda spoke, her voice was deflated. "They just headed out for a drive, hon. Listen, I'll have Tommy call you back tomorrow. I'm sure you want to get some sleep."

As if, Julie said to herself. She gritted her teeth. "Nice to catch up with you, Linda. Please have Tommy call me tomorrow. Love to you and Don." She couldn't wait to disconnect the call.

"Will do, hon. Don't work too hard."

Julie didn't respond, she just pressed the red button to end the call. So Tommy was definitely avoiding her, and she needed to go up to Jingle Valley.

***

Julie couldn't call Freddy, not at midnight, but she was wide awake. She'd pay the price for this insomnia tomorrow. Instead, she lay in bed and turned over disquieting thoughts in her mind. Like why Tommy hadn't told her how he was feeling. Or had he and she wasn't listening? Who was running the farm in his absence? She knew he had help, obviously, with all the cows and chickens, but how could he leave the place for weeks? Or more?

This was the family farm, the place her great-grandfather had started when he immigrated to America from Norway in 1915. She knew the family history. Kristoffer Olsen arrived in Boston and purchased 200 acres of farmland in western Massachusetts. He and his wife had four children, and their eldest, Arne, took over the farm after marrying Doris Brunetti, an Italian girl from Long Island who grew her own vegetables in the backyard. Arne and Doris had a son, Lars, and two daughters, Phyllis and Patricia. Doris died giving birth to Patricia and Lars moved away to grow corn in Iowa. Phyllis married Ben Tate, Julie's father, and they lived in the farmhouse with Arne until he died in 1985.

Julie was the youngest of Ben and Phyllis's five children. The first three came fast: Eric, Ella, and Don within four years. Then, when Don was twelve and Eric was already driving, Phyllis gave birth to Thomas, and three years later, Julie was born. Her mother was forty years old.

By the time Julie could walk, Eric was away at college and Ella was graduating high school. She and Tommy were naturally closer. When she was nine, Eric was already married and had kids nearly as old as Julie. After her father died, Julie always figured Eric would walk her down the aisle, but after Christopher broke it off and there was no one else to even consider as a possible groom, she pushed those thoughts aside, then further away. Besides, work was demanding. She made a great salary, but never moved from her little apartment in Chelsea. She usually brought her lunch to work and wore classic clothes that lasted for years. Generous with others and frugal to herself, Julie had saved two hundred thousand dollars by the time she was thirty.

***

The next morning, Julie slowed her pace as she reached the coffee shop two doors down from her office. She sucked in her stomach, then pulled on the door and stepped into a warm space redolent of vanilla and cinnamon. A young girl with spiky blue hair stood behind the counter and Julie let her stomach muscles relax.

"What can I get you, ma'am?"

Ugh. *Ma'am?* Julie tried not to roll her eyes before saying, "Large coffee, dark roast if you have it, please." Her stomach rumbled. "And one of those cinnamon buns, if you have any." She remembered them, probably had dreamt of them. Her holiday poundage would be in the double digits, for sure.

"Yeah, hang on." She leaned against the door leading into the kitchen. "Axel? I need the cinnamon things." She turned to fill a cardboard cup the size of a small bucket, and Julie tightened her abs again. He was here. He was making cinnamon buns in the kitchen. He had cute buns. He must smell so good.

And there he was, carrying a large metal tray of warm, sticky love. Involuntarily she let out a sigh. He looked up and smiled with recognition. "Good morning! Nice to see you're wearing your coat." Julie felt a flush heat her neck up to her cheeks.

"Morning. I couldn't resist the aroma," she said in a quivery voice that sounded like it belonged to someone else.

"That's the whole idea," he whispered conspiratorially. "These are fresh and warm from the oven." She watched as his long fingers detached one of the buns from the rest. He laid it on waxed paper and wrapped it carefully before placing it inside a paper bag.

The girl at the register rang up her order. "Seven twenty-five," she said dully, her eyes already on the new customer at the counter.

Julie handed her some bills and tossed the change into a large jar marked "TIPS." She hadn't noticed that jar the last time she was in the shop. The girl didn't even acknowledge the tip, and Julie wished she could stick her hand in there and take back the three quarters.

"What's your name?" Axel asked. She stepped off to the side, away from Blue Spiky Hair with an Attitude and the counter that had stood between them.

"Julie."

"Hi, Julie." He sure looked young. And so cute. This longing she felt in her gut, it was almost foreign, so long dormant that she barely recognized it.

"Hi, Axel." Something shifted when she said his name, maybe it was the ground.

"Are you staying in the city for the holidays?" He inched closer. She wanted to lick his neck, he smelled so sweet.

"I'm heading to my family's farm for Christmas. I already have my ticket." The holidays with a cute guy you don't even know – come on, Julie, she admonished silently. He hadn't invited her to do anything. Yet.

A question escaped her lips, one she never would have asked if she'd taken a moment to think about it.

"What are you doing New Year's Eve?" Oh God, how cheesy. Like that Ella Fitzgerald song, the one she heard Liz Callaway sing at Feinstein's last year.

"I'm not doing anything, other than working," he crooned. "But I close the shop at five. I know I should keep it open for all the drunken revelers, but I need some time off, right?" His eyes, so black and liquid. Oh, those eyes. Julie was ready to jump in. "Why, Julie, what are *you* doing New Year's Eve?"

"There's a party uptown. You could come with me," she shrugged, anticipating a rejection. Julie couldn't believe she'd asked him. She was never this forward with a guy. A young guy. And New Year's Eve!

"Sure." He glanced sideways at the line in front of the register. "I need to get back to work. Will you come in tomorrow, Julie?"

"I will. Axel." She sailed out of the shop.

***

Back in her office, she dialed Freddy's number, knowing he'd still be in bed.

"Mmmm?"

"Wake up, Frederick. I have news. Lots of it."

"Julie, we just said good-night, what, ten hours ago?"

"Yeah, well, listen to this." She gulped her coffee while the plump cinnamon bun lay uneaten on her desk. She wanted to fit into her best black dress on New Year's Eve.

"Alright, alright, but I need coffee," Freddy grumbled.

"Call me back," she said and disconnected. She picked up the cinnamon bun, still wrapped in waxed paper, and walked out of her office to lay it on Harmony's desk. Her assistant would be surprised to see it, but Julie knew she wouldn't pass it up. Harmony had more of a sweet tooth than even Julie had.

Her office phone rang. She picked it up, saying, "Provident Capital Management, Julie Tate here," and heard Freddy chuckle on the other end.

"Why didn't you call my cell?" she asked.

"Because I love the way you talk all professional on the other phone," he cackled. She heard him sip and swallow.

"Shut up. So listen." She filled him in on the message Thomas had left, adding that she'd called him in Phoenix and he'd been conveniently unavailable. "He went into hiding. What do you think's going on?"

"He flew the coop? Sorry, bad pun. I'd say he's probably stressed out. Jules, any sane man would go berserk working on a farm in the middle of nowhere."

"Apparently it's what he wanted. Freddy, this is so Tommy. I'm actually surprised he didn't do it sooner. When has he ever stuck with anything in his life? It's just that he never let on, to me at least, that he was unhappy. It was always, 'everything's great, Jules,' and 'life is good, Jules.' And now he wants to ditch the whole thing? This farm is our legacy, and he's abandoning it."

"Well, he won't talk to you, so you don't know all the facts. Are you still going up there for Christmas?"

"Yes. I have to. And I'm worried about what the place might look like. I haven't been up to visit since last Christmas, which is my fault. I should have been there more often. Maybe I'd have picked up on his attitude." She leaned back in her desk chair and trained her eye to the one piece of art on the walls of her office: a whimsical Maxwell Mays limited edition print called *Folk Art Farm*. It reminded her of Jingle Valley. "Freddy, come with me."

"Oh, honey, I can't. I promised my sister. You'll be fine. Call me when you get there. When's your train?"

"Wednesday at 7:20."

"Doll, you know that's too damn early for me. Hey, what other news did you have?"

"Oh!" Julie nearly knocked over the now-empty cardboard cup. "There's this guy who runs the coffee shop next door. Well, Harmony always got me my coffee in the past, but yesterday I went in, and the guy who runs it, or owns it, I don't know, well his name is Axel…"

"Slow down! Breathe in. That's it, Julie, take a deep breath. Axl? Like the Guns N' Roses guy?"

"Axel, yes, and I don't know if he was named after Axl Rose. Anyway, I invited him to the New Year's Eve party. I hope that's okay."

"Of course it's okay! My little Julie, all grown up. He must be cute for you to be so flustered."

"Yeah, he's pretty cute." She twirled a pen in her fingers, as if it was a baton and she was a majorette. When she tried to toss it in the air, it fell under her desk.

"For you, that means he's gorgeous."

Julie giggled, like she was thirteen again whispering to Tamara about Jason Hopkins. She cleared her throat. "Yeah, well. I asked him and he said sure."

"And you're leaving the city on Wednesday morning."

"Well, I might come back earlier than planned, especially since Tommy won't be there. But I have to see the farm, Freddy. I have to make sure it's not burned to the ground."

"And Axel will be here waiting."

"Shut up and goodbye." Julie turned to her computer monitor and opened a new message from Barton Thayer, one of two managing partners of the firm. Maxwell was already on vacation, no doubt bumping over moguls on Aspen Mountain. She scanned the lengthy message. Significant cutbacks, failure to bounce back, creditors, layoffs. Layoffs. Was PCM in trouble? Maxwell hadn't mentioned anything. They were a small operation, by New York standards, and Julie knew they'd been approached in the past by some of the larger financial houses. Maxwell and Barton had always managed to ward off the predators. She had a sizeable amount of PCM stock.

She picked up the phone and called her financial advisor.

THOMAS

Thomas enjoyed a swim before breakfast. Up and awake at four, he sat by the pool, waiting for the sunrise, thinking about Jingle Valley. And Julie. He dangled his feet, watching as the water, lit by lights embedded around the pool's perimeter, shimmered and undulated every time he moved.

It wasn't fair to her, he knew. She'd planned to take the train up for Christmas, and now, if she still went, she'd be alone while he was basking in the warm Phoenix weather. How would he tell her he wanted to move here? The farm was left to Julie and him by their father. The older siblings hadn't wanted anything to do with it, anyway, and they all inherited a fair share of his investments. But the farm was for Thomas and Julie. He wanted to sell it and split the profits with her. She'd have plenty of money. He'd have enough to build a new life out here in Arizona, maybe find a good woman, start a family. She should be grateful to him for figuring it all out. So why was he still afraid to have that conversation?

Thomas slid into the cool water and began doing laps. He worked his arms and shoulders as they knifed through the water. He counted thirty laps before he stopped to catch his breath, and as he rested his elbows on the concrete apron of the pool, he heard Linda's voice.

"Nice way to wake up, isn't it?" she called through the open kitchen window. She held a pot of coffee in one hand. "Come on in when you're ready." She pushed the window sash back down. It would be warm once the sun rose in the sky.

Thomas pulled himself up and out of the pool. He grabbed the towel he'd brought out with him and used it to absorb as much of the chlorinated water from his body as he could. A quick hot shower before dressing and he'd head into the main house.

Standing under the spray, he couldn't imagine a better life than this. A swim in the morning, and sun all day. A finer way to live than what he had at the farm. I just need to find a job, and an apartment, he reminded himself, but Don would help. He knows people here. He can open a few doors.

Thomas made his way across the patio to the back door and entered the kitchen. Morning sunlight streamed in through a skylight in the roof, illuminating Linda where she stood. His sister-in-law looked cool in a white cotton tunic over black leggings, her dark hair cropped short. She looked like that woman on television, the mom. Kardashian mom. Thomas remembered the day he met Linda. Don was stationed out west in the Air Force but flew home to introduce her to the family. Twelve-year-old Thomas was awestruck by her dark beauty, her fiery eyes. Her hair was long back then.

"Did you sleep well?" She poured coffee into two earthenware mugs and slid one across the counter to him.

"I slept great! This is like living in paradise." He savored the coffee, strong and black. It coursed through his veins like an illegal substance, giving him instant energy. He glanced up at Linda and noticed the dark smudges under her eyes. Thomas looked away.

"Well, winters are comfortable here, warmer than you're used to. Summers are pretty hot, though. A hundred plus." She poked the skin on his forearm. "You Tates are so white – you'd better wear sunblock every day." When she laughed, she tossed her head back slightly and Thomas could look right into her mouth. Lots of silver in there.

"You know any women who are single?"

Linda sat back on her barstool and regarded him. "You're only here for two weeks, Tommy. Are you just looking for a date for the holidays?"

Her eyes on him made Thomas squirm. He should tell her his plans. What was he afraid of? She wasn't going to kick him out of the pool house. What had Don told her?

He leaned forward, resting those white forearms on the beige granite countertop, feeling its cold smoothness under his skin. "I want to move here. Live in Arizona for good. I talked to Don about it last night and I'm ready to make this permanent. Start a new life." He stopped when he realized he was babbling.

Linda sipped her coffee and said nothing for a moment. When she set her mug back on the counter, she asked, "What about the farm? Are you going to sell it?"

Thomas nodded. "Yeah, that's the plan. I need to talk to Julie. And I know it's going to be a hard conversation." He stared into his nearly-empty mug.

"So Julie doesn't know. And that's why you avoided the phone call last night." Thomas picked up nothing from her voice, but when he raised his eyes, he could see Linda's jaw was set, her eyes dark and fiery. With dark circles under them that Thomas could only guess came from lack of sleep.

He shrugged, a dismissal of sorts. "She knows I've been unhappy. Look, Julie's got a real big job in New York City. She doesn't want to run a farm. But we own the place together, and I need her blessing to sell. She's…she's got a lot of emotional attachment to the place."

"Well, you'd better call her today." Linda pushed back and stood, ending their conversation. "Help yourself to anything in the fridge. And to answer your question, Tommy, I know plenty of nice young women." She turned and walked away.

JULIE

Julie packed for what would amount to five days at Jingle Valley. With still no word from Tommy, she fumed as she rolled shirts and jeans into her travel bag. The nerve! She would not allow him to abandon the family farm. Her older brothers had no interest, and her sister Ella in San Diego rarely communicated with any of them, other than an emailed photo card at Christmas. There were seventeen years between Ella and Julie, and they'd never really lived together in the same house, but still. Tommy, to whom she was closest, had run off to Arizona and was hiding out at Don and Linda's. If she could have taken the week off, she'd fly out there and confront him in person.

She'd given Axel her phone number and told him she'd be back on Monday. He'd texted her an hour earlier and wished her a safe trip and a happy Christmas. She wondered if he celebrated, if he had family. She wished they'd known each other well enough that she could invite him up to Dalton with her, to keep her warm in the big farmhouse. As she tossed underwear on top of her clothes, she pictured the two of them in front of the big stone fireplace, the one her great-grandfather had built from stones he pulled out of the ground. She fingered the silk of a camisole and let her mind wander. Axel. He could get so lucky with her. She'd need to exercise some restraint with him on New Year's Eve, not act so desperate, even though it had been months.

Her phone rang just as she zipped her bag, and when she saw it was Tommy calling, she paused. She couldn't not take the call; they needed to have this conversation. She pressed a button to answer.

"Tommy." She said his name as if it was sour milk in her mouth.

"Hey, Jules. What's up?"

"Cut it out. What the hell are you doing?"

"Trying to live a life that I don't hate. I can't do the farm game anymore, Jules."

"So you said on that cowardly phone message. You cannot abandon the farm, Tommy."

"I know, I know. I'm gonna put it up for sale. We'll make a decent profit, Jules, and split it right down the middle. That's what Mom and Dad wanted for us."

"Really. Well, I have a say in this whole thing, you know." She sat on her bed, then stood up and paced to the window. Darkness fell early in December, and she imagined her brother lounging in the sun.

"Why wouldn't you agree? It's not like you'd ever want to live at the place. Julie, you came up once last year, as if it was an obligation. Why do you care if the place is sold?"

"It's the family farm, Tommy! For generations. From our great-grandfather, who by the way you probably don't even know his name. "

"Olsen," he said quietly.

Julie was silent, refusing to acknowledge that he actually knew, or that he had made a very valid point about her interest in Jingle Valley. She dropped to the bed again. "It's just, I don't know, all the memories. Where we spent our childhood. Remember the tree house? Remember picking strawberries? Why do you want to live in the desert?"

"I'm tired of being cold. And I'm tired of being alone. I can't meet anyone out there, Jules. I want to have a family. You can understand that, can't you?"

Julie's throat constricted with his words. Of course she could understand. Seeing Christopher had brought it all back. Julie the old maid. She had no husband, no children, but a hell of a good-paying job, and now she wondered about the financial health of her company. The youngest Tate, the spinster, the one her siblings would pity. She swallowed down the image. Tommy wanted a family. Of course she could understand.

"Jules, you still there?"

"I'm here," she whispered. *Barely.* "Why Phoenix?"

"It's sweet out here. I'll be close to Don and Linda. Eric's coming in tonight from Austin. And Ella's not even that far away."

Julie blinked hard. *Everyone together on the west coast, everyone but me.* But wait a minute, a tiny voice inside her head nudged. *Why shouldn't Tommy find his happiness? Why shouldn't you?* She cleared her throat, hoping her voice would be strong when she spoke.

"Okay, well, good for you. Really, Tommy, I mean it. But nothing's going up for sale just yet. I'm still heading to the farm for Christmas. I leave in the morning. We can talk about this after I get back." If she agreed to the sale, she'd spend one last Christmas in her childhood home. She'd make as many memories as she could.

"Yeah, sure. I'm surprised you're still going, though."

"Without you there? I'll be fine, Tommy." Alone and just swell. "Talk to you later."

"Merry Christmas, little sister," he whispered into the phone, but Julie had already disconnected.

***

Even at the early hour, Julie's train was crowded. She found a seat by the window and lifted her bag to the rack above it. Shrugging off her jacket, she folded it and laid it atop her bag, then settled into her seat. She had a cardboard cup of coffee from the place next to her apartment, although she'd have gladly walked the twelve blocks to see Axel one more time. That would have been ridiculous, though, and she didn't want to appear desperate. Even if she was.

An older woman asked if the seat next to her was empty.

"Yes, of course," said Julie, hoping her new neighbor wasn't chatty.

"Would you like some shortbread? I can't say I made it myself, but it's good." She pried the lid from a red-and-black plaid tin and held it out to Julie.

"Oh, thanks, thanks very much," Julie said, picking up a wedge. "This will be perfect with my coffee."

"My pleasure," said the woman, who introduced herself as Hilda. She took a piece for herself and replaced the cover, then tucked the tin back into a large cloth bag on the floor at her feet.

"I'm Julie. Where are you headed?" Great, now I'm the chatty one, Julie said to herself. It'll serve me right if this lady prattles on for the whole journey. The price you pay for a piece of buttery shortbread.

"Saratoga Springs," said Hilda. Her hands were wrinkled and brown-spotted, but her nails were painted in candy cane stripes of red and white. Those will be my hands in a few years, Julie thought. Why do I always forget sunblock? "I'm visiting with my son for the holidays. How about you?"

"I'm getting off in Albany. Then it's an hour's drive to Dalton, in Massachusetts."

"Visiting family as well?"

"Yes," Julie said. "Thank you again for the shortbread." She reached into her purse and pulled out her Kindle. Fortunately, her seatmate had the same idea, opening a paperback book.

They rode in silence, Julie lost in a new novel. When they reached Albany, she had to wake Hilda so she could exit the train.

"Oh! Trains always make me sleepy," she said with a laugh. The older woman stood up slowly, using the seat's back for leverage. "And I'm a turtle these days. Aging isn't for sissies." A shadow passed over Hilda's gray eyes.

"Well, don't miss your stop," Julie said, hoisting her bag to her shoulder and holding her jacket in her free arm. "Merry Christmas."

"You as well, dear. I hope you have a memorable stay." Hilda rested her hand on Julie's arm and Julie had an urge to hug her. But she didn't.

It'll be a memorable stay, all right, Julie said to herself as she stepped down to the platform.

***

After wrangling with the rental agency about her reservation (worthy of a Seinfeld episode), Julie drove out to Route 20 and an hour later crossed into Massachusetts. She skirted the state forest through Pittsfield and left the city behind as she headed toward the farm. The area had changed since she was a girl – now there were strip malls and drive-through coffee shops, more houses where there used to be acres of open space. The road lifted her higher above the valley. And as she rounded a bend, with tall pine trees on her right, there it was, magnificent in her eye. She couldn't imagine why Tommy had felt he had to flee. There was a hint of snow on the ground, not much, just enough to add magic to the landscape, and as she descended into the valley the weathered barn stood tall against a clear blue sky. Julie gripped the steering wheel and hummed along to the radio. *Jingle bells swing and jingle bells ring.* She parked the car in the open garage stall, next to Tommy's black Silverado truck. She grabbed her bag and walked up the gravel drive to the side door of the house. No one ever used the front door. The key was right where Tommy said it would be and Julie smiled at the idea that around here, he could still hide a key under a painted rock. He probably could have left the house unlocked, for that matter. She opened the door and stepped into the big kitchen. And stopped.

It was as if someone had been baking. Apple pie. Julie breathed in deeply. Her mom always made apple pies for Christmas – three of them. She laid her hand on the stove. It was cold. The counters were spotless, the floor clean. Well, at least Tommy was neat. She opened the refrigerator. There was a pint of light cream, five eggs, and a block of sharp cheddar cheese. A six-pack of beer, one missing. She shut the door and opened the freezer. Ha! A carton of chocolate ice cream, and one of cherry vanilla. Good ol' Tommy. There was also a roast, wrapped in clear plastic, and some frozen vegetables. She took out the roast and set it on the counter. It might be thawed by tomorrow; otherwise, she'd be ordering pizza from the only place that delivered.

Julie walked from the kitchen into the dining room. The same polished oak table used by her parents dominated the space. A mismatched china cabinet stood against one wall. Everything looked the same, just as it had when she was a coltish teenager twenty years ago. How could he let this go? How could *she*?

A clock's chime broke the silence, the sixteen-note Westminster tune. Then two strikes for the hour. She wondered if she should try the little market in town. They used to stay open until six on Christmas Eve. She headed back into the kitchen and screamed when she saw a figure at the door. Without opening it, and hoping the man didn't realize the door was unlocked, she called out, "What do you want?"

He waved at her through the glass. "I'm Ethan Webb, from next door," he shouted. He looked friendly enough, and Julie didn't think he was lying. But, next door? There wasn't another house in sight.

"I'm Julie, Tommy's sister," she said, quietly lifting her fingers to the latch and turning it as she looked at the man's face through the glass. He could easily break the window in the door and grab her by the throat. She took a step back.

"Is Thomas here?" She realized no one called her brother Tommy.

"Um, no. Not right now." She had no idea whether he'd told anyone his plans. And she wasn't going to do it for him, or let this stranger know that she was here, alone.

"Oh. He won't be around for Christmas?" Ethan ran his hand through thin hair, pushing it back from a broad forehead.

"Um," Julie faltered. "Sure. Of course he will be." Julie kept this kind-looking man standing on her doorstep, but she couldn't let him in.

Ethan peered at her through the window, and Julie saw his eyes rest on the frozen roast. "Oh, you've got plans for Christmas Day then," he shouted. "My wife and I were about to invite Thomas – well, you and Thomas – to our house for dinner." He had an accent she couldn't place, but he definitely wasn't from around here.

"Oh! How kind. Where do you live again?"

"Just up the road. Yellow house on the left. We bought the land from Pete Crane," Ethan said.

The Cranes. Julie remembered. Pete and Joyce Crane had a Christmas tree farm where Julie's dad always got the family's tree. None of their kids wanted to continue the business, and the land went up for sale a couple of years ago. She unlocked the door and opened it.

"Mr. Webb, Thomas won't be back tomorrow. It's just me." She watched his face.

"Well then, you're definitely coming to our house tomorrow. My wife Pauline cooks enough for an army, so you can't say no." He grinned, a gap between his two front teeth that on Ethan looked endearing. "And please, call me Ethan."

Julie nodded and said, "Okay, sure. I'll come. What time?"

"Dinner is at one. Come at noon. That's what I was told to say." He finally smiled. "You do look a lot like Thomas. Who's older?"

"He is, by a year," Julie said. "Can I bring something tomorrow?" She almost laughed at the absurdity of her question. A carton of ice cream or a frozen roast, what's your pleasure?

"Nah, just bring yourself. And dress comfortable. We don't do fancy at our house."

Thank goodness for that, since she hadn't packed anything fancy. But the word reminded her of Axel and New Year's Eve. She'd better not gorge herself tomorrow. Ethan stuck his hands in his coat pockets and turned to leave.

"Thanks for the invitation, Ethan. It was very kind."

Ethan stepped back outside into the cold and turned back to Julie. "The yellow house on the left. You can't miss it! Nice to meet you, Julie," said Ethan, offering his hand.

She took it and was surprised by its softness. Ethan didn't do farm work, Julie thought.

THOMAS

Eric was due to arrive sometime in the afternoon. Apparently when he visited, about twice a year, he always stayed in Thomas's nephew Tyler's old room. Thomas didn't really mind being in the guest house, but he wondered why he wasn't offered a room in the house. After all, there were three empty bedrooms since the kids had all moved out. Plenty of space. At the same time, he enjoyed his solitude, so he let it go.

That was a difficult conversation with Julie. And now she'd be at Jingle Valley. Alone, he imagined, unless she managed to get one of her girlfriends to go with her. Or her friend Freddy, that character. He'd feel less guilty knowing she wasn't up there alone for Christmas. Maybe he should call Ethan and ask him to check in on her. Ethan didn't even know Thomas was in Phoenix, and Thomas hadn't shared his plans about relocating with him.

And Julie might not be willing to sell. Thomas mulled that over as he reclined on the firm mattress. She'd have to buy him out then. Thomas assumed she had the money, but why would she? She knew nothing about running a dairy farm, and she had no inclination to learn, at least she'd never shown any.

"Tommy boy!" Eric's booming voice carried across the patio into the guest house. Thomas lifted his body off the bed before Eric could catch him lazing about and walked outside, into the bear hug welcome of his oldest brother.

Eric had gained a ton of weight, Thomas noted. Plenty of good barbecue in Texas.

"Bro," Thomas said against his brother's massive chest. "Good to see you."

Eric pulled back to look at his youngest brother. "Donny here tells me you thinkin' 'bout leavin' the farm behind and movin' out west. That true?" His pink face looked like a boiled ham. With little squinty raisin eyes.

"Thinking about it, yeah. I've had enough snow and cold. I could use a better climate. Maybe settle down, start a family."

"Well, you better get a move on, boy! No time like now. Hell, I had my kids early, now they're all grown and moved away. How old are you now? Forty?"

"Thirty-six, Eric. I still have time."

"Well, hell, even I still got time, but you know, snip snip, no worries for ol' Eric, ha ha ha."

"So, Margaret couldn't come with you?" Thomas knew that Eric and his wife were having problems, but now he was in the mood to needle his brother.

Eric wiped his forehead with his hand, then pressed his palm against his trouser leg, leaving a faint impression. "Nah, she wanted to visit her mother in Tampa. Ya know, her mom's ninety."

"Ah." Thomas had heard Don and Linda talking about Eric's secretary-slash-mistress, a woman named Sandy. "Well, you tell Margaret I'm sorry I missed seeing her."

"Yeah," Eric mumbled, staring at the shimmering aquamarine water of the swimming pool. Thomas pictured him doing a belly flop into the pool, displacing half the water and infuriating Linda. He grinned at the image in his mind.

"Well, it's good to see you, bro." Thomas realized he had absolutely nothing to talk about with Eric. Maybe it was the age difference. When Thomas was ten, Eric was already married with a couple of kids. He'd moved to Washington, D.C., had some kind of job with the federal government, then moved to Austin about twenty-five years ago and gotten in on the ground floor of an internet-based business, and made a ton of money along the way. Thomas had never visited him in Austin, but Eric sent photos of his house once, an enormous villa in the Westlake hills. He had a nine-car garage. Eric had never been back to the farm, not even once, and from what Thomas could ascertain, he had no interest in it whatsoever. He wouldn't care what Thomas and Julie did with the property. Julie was the only one who mattered.

And Eric never even asked about Julie. She may be nineteen years younger, but she was still his sister. And yet, Thomas didn't bring her up, either. It was too hard to talk about her right now.

"Listen, I think I'll take a dip. How about you?" Thomas figured he could escape in the pool. Eric would never be able to swim laps with him.

"Nah, maybe later, Tommy. I'm a-gonna head back inside and see what Linda's puttin' together."

Thomas pulled off his shirt, noting Eric's glance at his lean physique, his chiseled abs. Hey, it took work,

Thomas thought, pleased he had at least one thing over his fat rich brother.

"Okay, catch ya later," Thomas said before jumping into the pool. It was only about seventy degrees outside, but the pool water was heated to a bath-like seventy-eight, according to the thermometer by the diving board.

Thomas swam twenty laps, then pulled himself out of the pool and lay on a lounge chair, letting the warm winter sun dry him off. Christmas Eve and he was in his swim trunks, lying in the sun. It didn't get much better than this, he thought.

JULIE

Julie called Freddy at eight o'clock on Christmas Eve.

"Is it a bad time?"

"It's never a bad time for you, doll! My niece is still up, but she's losing steam. How are you? How's the farm? And…the chickens?"

"Everything looks okay from what I can see. A neighbor stopped by and invited me to dinner tomorrow, so I guess I won't be alone."

"And that's a good thing! You have neighbors up there? I'm surprised."

Julie heard laughter and the sound of glasses clinking in the background.

"He's half a mile up the road, but that's considered a neighbor. He was really nice. And before you ask, he's married. I'm joining him and his family. Freddy, I don't want to keep you from all the festivities."

He groaned. "Please! You've given me a respite. So how about Tommy? Did you talk with him?"

"He finally called me back. Said he was tired of being cold and he can't meet anyone in Dalton."

"Well, join the club, Sir Thomas," said Freddy.

Julie laughed. "Yeah, that's what I should have said. But he sounded serious, Freddy. I think he really means to stay in Arizona. He wants to sell the farm."

"No kidding? Do you have a say in this? Aren't you part owner?"

"I am and I do, actually. Our parents bequeathed the farm to Tommy and me equally. Our older siblings were taken care of, and they have no argument about it, as far as I know. But Tommy can't sell this place without my consent."

"And do you consent?"

Julie was silent.

"Jules, you still there?"

"I'm here," she said softly. "And I don't know, Freddy. This place has been in my family for generations. I hate the thought of it being sold."

"But you don't want to run a farm, do you?"

"Of course not. I can't. But Freddy, when I walked into the house this afternoon, I could swear I smelled apple pie. As if my mother was there. It was surreal." And why did it matter so much? She couldn't answer her own question. She just knew that she couldn't let go.

"It's just your memory, love. Memory can be powerful. And you haven't been up there for ages."

"I'm hoping I can find an answer while I'm here. Maybe a sign that I should hang onto it, maybe a sign that I should sell it. I just can't think about selling it. So maybe I'd be blind to that kind of a sign. Oh God, I'm prattling. Hey, go back to everyone before little Madison falls asleep."

"Listen, sweetie, tonight you should relax, have a glass of wine, get a good night's rest. You're probably exhausted, and you have to interact with strange farm people tomorrow. I'll call you tomorrow evening."

"Thanks, Freddy. Merry Christmas."

"Merry Christmas, Julie."

***

Julie awoke Christmas morning with a sense of wonder. She slept in her old bedroom, knowing Tommy would have prepared it for her arrival. Nestled between clean sheets and warmed by three quilts, she opened her eyes as a weak sun lifted in a pale blue sky.

In the distance, she heard church bells and knew they belonged to the white steeple up the hill. She should make a stop there this morning. After all, it was Christmas and she hadn't been to church in a very long time. She threw back the covers and shivered. The heat was kept low, just enough to keep the pipes from freezing, so it was cold in the old house. She pulled on an extra sweatshirt and stuck her sock-covered feet into scuff slippers that she'd found in her closet. They weren't hers, and Julie wondered if they belonged to someone who used to sleep over.

She made coffee, grateful for the cream in the fridge, and scooped out chocolate ice cream. Hey, better to have it for breakfast, she thought, figuring she'd walk up the hill to church. She had no idea when services were held, but she'd make the trek anyway, even if only for the exercise and fresh air. But first she'd walk around the property. Her property. Tommy had said his farm workers would take care of feeding the animals while he was away, and she hoped that was true, because Julie had no knowledge about feeding or milking. As a young girl, she generally stayed clear of the farm work, as much as she loved being around her father. She preferred learning from her mother in the kitchen, watching her cook and bake. Julie smiled, thinking that she never even used those skills anymore. She bet she could make a giant cinnamon bun as delicious as the ones Axel made.

Axel. She hoped he wouldn't forget about her. On impulse, she grabbed her phone and composed a Christmas text message to him.

Merry Christmas! It's cold here on the farm. Hope you're keeping warm. See you soon.

Before she could second-guess herself, she hit send. And the text was on its merry way.

She poured coffee and enjoyed the first satisfying sip. Ping! Text message back.

Cold and lonely here. Is it NYE yet?

Julie shivered. Oh, the anticipation. So he was looking forward to New Year's Eve, too. Maybe she should return earlier than Monday. *For what, Julie?* This is casual, flirty. She stared at her phone and began typing.

I wish! Returning on Monday. Will stop in to see you. Can't wait.

There. That didn't seem too desperate. Casual and flirty.

She waited, sipped coffee and stared at her silent phone. Ping!

Cant wait either. Xx

Oh. Xx. Kiss kiss right back at you, Axel baby. She didn't respond. That was good enough. She dug into the bowl of ice cream.

After pulling on black boots, red mittens, and her winter jacket, Julie headed outside. Cold! The chill breath of winter whispered against her cheek. She crunched through a thin layer of snow on the ground and walked toward the big barn. All the animals were inside, warm and dry.

There was no one around, but a piece of paper stuck on a nail in the barn wall told her the guy who came to feed the cows and chickens had been here and left. "Pete C. 12/25 5:40AM" was scrawled on the paper. It was Christmas morning and she didn't expect to see workers today. As long as the animals were taken care of. Julie knew she couldn't run a dairy farm. But could she buy Tommy's half and have others run it for her? There was a lot of land here, nearly a thousand acres. Sweeping fields to the foothills of the Berkshire Mountains. Land was valuable now, and she knew Tommy had turned down brokers looking to develop those acres into neighborhoods or strip malls.

She turned and headed in the opposite direction, following the sound of the church bells from the white-spired church on the hill above Jingle Valley. Her grandfather had named this place. His father, Kristoffer Olsen, had simply called it Olsen Farm, but her grandfather, Arne Olsen, heard jingle bells one Christmas morning and told his father the farm should be called Jingle Valley. And apparently old Kristoffer agreed. Jingle Valley Farm was born. Julie loved the magic of the name. It was as if Christmas lived here all year round. Her mother used to sell handmade Christmas ornaments from the house - brightly-painted wooden hearts cut with a jigsaw by her father, and braided loaves of lighter-than-air yeast bread, spiced with cardamom and dusted with sugar and almonds. Tourists on their way to Stockbridge or Lenox would stop at the farm after seeing the sign on Route 20 advertising fresh eggs or homemade honey or Grandma's Christmas Shop. There was another sign at the end of their long driveway, directing them down the long dirt road. Julie often greeted them, when she wasn't in school. Her mom would come out from the kitchen, wiping her hands on a brightly-colored apron, and direct them to the open stall in the garage where she kept jars of clover honey, peach preserves, and the wooden hearts, decorated for whatever season was appropriate.

Eventually, business slackened. People didn't want to make a detour off the Mass Pike, not when they could stop at a McDonald's right on the side of the highway.

Julie arrived at the church, but there was no one outside, so she opened the heavy door as quietly as she could and slipped into the vestibule. This was the Congregational church, and the last time she'd been inside had been for someone's wedding when she was about twelve years old. She remembered seeing the bride, whose father was a policeman in town (*what was their name?*). Ella had come back to the farm to be a bridesmaid, and Julie was allowed to go to the church, to see her big sister dressed in a dusty rose dress with matching shoes, a big flower stuck in her curly hair. Ella looked miserable, but the bride was gorgeous, as Julie recalled. Slim and beaming, she glittered in a dazzling white gown. Julie's mother said strapless wasn't appropriate for a wedding, but it was the style. Julie was mesmerized by the bride that day, the image seared into her memory.

Twenty-two years later, as she stepped into the church, Julie could still picture that bride. There weren't many people present this Christmas Day, and she learned later that the Christmas Eve service was the bigger draw. There was a Catholic church in Pittsfield, a Lutheran church farther down the road where the Tates had worshipped, and a New Life Assembly of God building that Julie spotted on her drive yesterday.

After twenty minutes of silent meditation, she rose and slipped out of the church as quietly as she had come in. She was due at Ethan's house at noon, and needed to bring something with her. Of course, nothing was open today, but maybe she could find a bottle of wine in the house. She knew Tommy preferred beer, but maybe he had a bottle lying around somewhere. Either that or the unopened carton of cherry vanilla ice cream.

THOMAS

Thomas slept later than usual on Christmas morning. Perhaps his body had adjusted to the two-hour time difference, or maybe it was all those laps in the pool. Or maybe he was just trying to avoid spending time with Eric. His two older brothers had a lot more in common: rich, successful, driven. Thomas never considered himself lazy or unambitious, but compared to these two, he felt like a slug. And he wasn't. Which was why he stayed in the pool until his skin was shriveled.

Linda had joined him last night, sleek in a one-piece black tank suit. She kept herself in pretty good shape, he noticed.

"Nothing like a swim on Christmas Eve, huh, Tommy?" Linda glistened in the moonlight.

"It's great," he said, treading water at the deep end.

"You know, living here, it's not like being on vacation."

"I know. I'd have to find a job. I know all of it, but I still want to make the change." He watched Eric and Don smoke cigars at the far end of the yard. They were oblivious to Linda and him.

"I invited a few friends over tomorrow afternoon. We keep Christmas casual, but it's our tradition to open up the house to neighbors and friends. Anyone who wants to stop by is welcome."

Thomas raised his eyebrows. "That's great. So, who's coming?"

Linda smiled big, her teeth too small for her mouth. "There'll be some nice women there, Tommy. I told them about you already."

"You did? What did you say, exactly?" Please don't tell them I'm a farmer from New England, he implored silently.

"I said you're Don's younger brother, and thinking about moving here. The rest is up to you." She ducked her head under the water and swam in a straight line toward the other end. Thomas raised his elbows to rest on the pool's rim and watched her swim, a seal in the water. She could stay under for almost the entire length of the pool. When she resurfaced at his end, she laughed. "Merry Christmas!" And flip, she was gone again.

Thomas hoisted himself up and sat on the edge, letting his feet swirl the aqua water. He wanted a life like this, a swim at night in the open air, a warm sun during the day. He wanted this more than anything he could ever remember wanting.

JULIE

Julie found a bottle of red wine in a cupboard next to the refrigerator. There was a rooster on the label, a Shiraz from 2009. She didn't know wine well enough, but hoped it would be an acceptable gift. She brushed her hair and re-applied makeup. She wanted to make a good impression on Ethan and his family. But she decided to drive up to the house. She knew these people - someone says the house is a half-mile up the road and she could be walking for an hour. She hopped in her rental car and pulled away from the house.

Ethan didn't lie. The house was a half-mile up the road, and you couldn't miss that bright yellow exterior. She parked far enough away from the house that other cars could have space, and she'd be able to leave without being blocked in. Grabbing the bottle of wine, she walked with purpose toward the front door, which sported a festive wreath of pinecones and red bows. She pressed the doorbell and waited. Nothing. After a minute, she pressed again. Nothing. Did they not hear her? She knocked, hard enough to hurt her knuckles.

She was about to turn around and leave when the door was flung open and a boy of about ten stood looking up at her.

"Merry Christmas!" he chirped. "I don't know you."

"Merry Christmas to you, too!" Julie said in reply. "I'm Julie, from Jingle Valley Farm."

"That's Mr. Tate's farm."

"I'm Mr. Tate's sister. Ms. Tate." Perhaps she shouldn't call herself by her first name. Some parents didn't want their children calling adults by their first name. Her friend Jess was adamant that her kids use Auntie Julie or Ms. Tate when speaking, never just Julie.

"Okay, you can come in," he said and Julie tried not to laugh. Cute kid.

He led the way into a room filled with people, and she scanned the crowd, desperate to find Ethan.

"Julie! So glad you could make it!" Ethan was behind her, his arms outstretched. She allowed him to hug her.

"Merry Christmas! And thank you so much for inviting me." She held out the bottle of wine, with a red bow taped to its neck. She had rummaged around in the same closet where her mother had always kept paper and ribbon, and sure enough, there was a red bow. "This is for you."

Ethan stared at the bottle. His cheeks flushed.

"I'm sorry, do you not drink wine? I should have asked," she said, nearly smacking herself on the forehead.

"No, it's fine," he said with a chuckle. "Did you find this in the house?" His eyes reflected the tiny white lights strung all around the living room.

How would he know that, Julie thought. "Yes, I did," she stammered. "I didn't know I'd be coming for dinner, and I didn't have a chance to pick anything up."

"It's fine, Julie. Really," Ethan said, the color in his face returning to its normal shade. "I gave this bottle to Thomas a few months ago. Guess he's not a wine drinker. But it's a good wine, so let's enjoy it." Now it was Julie's turn to blush.

"I feel like an idiot," she whispered.

"Nonsense. Come on, I'll introduce you. First, to my better half." He led her into the kitchen, where a woman stood at a counter, arranging covered dishes. The kitchen was huge, with one of those islands in the middle that had its own sink. The woman looked up from her task.

"Hon, this is Julie Tate, Thomas's sister. I told you about her. Julie, this is my wife Pauline."

Pauline used her forearm to push back strands of hair and smiled at Julie. Julie recognized that weary holiday smile – it was the way her mom looked on Christmas Day, after cleaning and cooking and baking and wrapping. "Merry Christmas, Julie. We're happy you could join us. So sorry to hear Thomas couldn't be here this year."

"Yes, I was sorry, too. And thank you so much for the invitation," she said, casting her eyes at Ethan, "you kept me from spending Christmas Day all by myself." She realized how pathetic that sounded, and added, "Although I have plenty of ice cream to keep me company. Um…have you lived here long?"

"No, we just moved in last June. Had this house built for us. We left Albany so we could raise the kids outside the city."

"I can understand that," Julie said, remembering her own happy childhood. "So, how can I help?"

"I'm just about done. It's buffet-style, the only way we could pull this off," Pauline said in a chalky voice. Well, of course she's exhausted, Julie told herself. She's got a dozen kids and as many adults in her house. There were sixteen chairs at the long table in the dining room, which extended into the living room, and various small tables set up around the first floor of the house. Fortunately, the kitchen was big enough to hold the six people who were in it at the time, without everyone bumping into each other.

Ethan, full of energy, let everyone know that they could eat whenever they wanted. Some people rose immediately and headed into the kitchen. Julie stepped aside; she wasn't really hungry anyway. Ethan kissed his wife's cheek, then picked up a carving knife and set to work on the turkey. Julie liked these people, and wanted to stay close.

"So, Ethan, you said you brought this bottle of wine to Tommy a few months back. What was the occasion?"

Ethan had crinkles around his eyes, easy crinkles and a ready smile. "We'd just moved in, and Thomas invited us to dinner. We brought the bottle with us then."

"He cooked for you?" Julie was incredulous. She never knew her brother as a cook, knowing he preferred take-out and pizza from Pizza's, the only place in town. It was a wonder he stayed so fit, but she attributed it to the manual labor he did every day.

"No, Sarah did the cooking. Do you know Zack and Sarah?" Julie shook her head. "You'll meet them. Nice kids. They live in the cottage on your property."

Julie's grandfather had built the cottage in the 1950s to house seasonal farm workers. It was a simple place, basically a bunkhouse, but with a small kitchen and bathroom. And a giant fireplace that heated the entire space.

"They're what some folks would call hippies, you know? Kind of living off the land." Ethan leaned closer. "But they're very nice. That Sarah, she can cook! Made us a wonderful dinner and baked an apple pie, too."

"Are they here?" Julie twisted to look into the dining room.

"Nope, I invited them to come over, but they said they liked the quiet. I'm thinking the idea of twenty-odd folks in this house mighta scared 'em off." Ethan chuckled. "They like to keep to themselves."

"Well, I'll swing by later this afternoon to say hello."

"That'd be right nice, Julie. I'm sure they'll take to you the same way they did to Thomas." He held out the bottle of wine. "Why don't you take this to them?" He winked.

"What? You're regifting my regift?"

"Offer it to Zack and Sarah. If they don't want it, they'll probably just pass it off to Thomas. Or Pauline and me. This bottle might become the wine no one ever really drinks."

THOMAS

Christmas in Phoenix was casual and laid-back, with a decidedly Southwestern flair. Macaroni and cheese with chorizo and chiles. Mushroom and chile tacos. Chipotle, bean, and beef chili. And plenty of tequila. Too much tequila; Thomas couldn't keep up with Eric and Don. He shouldn't have even tried. But when he woke up the following morning and couldn't recall the name of the woman lying next to him in bed, his head pounded even more. Shit. What's her name? He shut his eyes against the morning light that streamed through a curtainless window. Her purse. Thomas opened his eyes and scanned the room. There, on the floor next to the door. If he could look at her driver's license. She didn't stir. Should he wait until she went into the bathroom? God, if she caught him going through her purse…

A hand on his bare hip made him flinch. Thomas rolled onto his back and the hand traveled.

"Good morning," she murmured, tangled hair covering part of her face, a knotty web of coffee-colored strands. He did remember that she was pretty, and oh, the body, soft and pillowy where it should be.

"Hey, beautiful. Good morning," he replied. Natalie? Nora? Crap. "You okay this morning?"

"Absolutely," she purred, nestling in closer, playing *Reveille* with her fingertips.

Man oh man, Thomas thought, this is like a sitcom episode. Mulva? Dolores? Not Dolores.

She ducked under the covers and Thomas thought 'honey' was just fine.

JULIE

Julie didn't stay too long at the Webbs' after eating, not just because she wanted to meet Zack and Sarah, but she knew if she stayed she'd eat more pie. *Axel Axel Axel*, she kept repeating to herself. *Little black dress.* Maybe not even the dress. She'd walk and run and walk and run all around the farm. Cardio. Burn off those calories.

Julie had to smile. She liked Ethan and Pauline a lot. Nice family, good neighbors. There was something special about living in this area. She'd inhabited her apartment for almost nine years and she still only knew the name of the guy who lived next door. Jason Stern. And that was only because he'd asked her to water his plants and feed his cat when he went to Israel two years ago. They remained on good terms. But the other tenants? Outside of a muttered 'good morning' in the lobby, she didn't even know their names, and she probably wouldn't recognize them if they passed on the street.

She left the house and drove around the perimeter of the farm, heading toward the little cottage on the far end of the property. A whisper of smoke rose from the stone chimney, unwavering in the cold, windless air, a straight line up to the heavens. Julie parked the car and grabbed the bottle of wine from the passenger seat. The front door of the cottage was decorated with a lovely evergreen wreath, bright with pinecones and holly berries. Tommy hadn't put up a wreath.

Julie knocked on the front door and it opened wide. She stared up into the dark face of a tall man with broad shoulders.

"Greetings," he said in a baritone voice.

"Hi, I'm Julie, Tommy's sister." She caught herself too late. Everyone here called him Thomas. "Thomas Tate."

"Come on in," he said, stepping aside to let her enter.

"This is for you," Julie said, offering the wine. Zack stared at the bottle before accepting it with a nod. "I don't know if you drink wine…"

"Sure. Thanks much," he said. Julie had a feeling the bottle would be traveling again.

She looked around and nodded with appreciation. No longer a bunkhouse for seasonal farmhands, the cottage was now a charming home. There was a glowing fire in the stone hearth, with orange flames reaching up into the chimney.

"Sarah!" he called out and Julie heard a door close softly.

Sarah was petite, small like a girl not yet fully grown. A short yellow braid stuck out the back of her head and she wore an oversized black sweatshirt with a green and silver sequined Christmas tree on it. Julie took two steps forward and offered her hand.

"Hi, Sarah. I'm Julie, Thomas's sister."

Sarah took Julie's hand in both of her own small hands, and Julie felt a rush of warmth, like a gust out of the fireplace.

"Older sister or younger sister?" She didn't let go of Julie's hand.

"Younger. I'm the baby of the family," Julie said, withdrawing her hand reluctantly.

Sarah was striking in her simplicity. Flawless skin like fine porcelain with no marks or lines. Gray-blue eyes and unplucked, natural brows on her tiny face, and when she smiled, Julie could see she had straight teeth that were the color of teeth, not artificially-whitened teeth that everyone in Manhattan seemed to have.

Zack was dark-skinned, with unruly black hair and a beard that reached his shirt collar. He looked like a mountain man, a giant who moved with the grace of a dancer.

"Would you like some tea?" Sarah asked.

"Thank you. That would be lovely."

Zack still held the bottle of wine. He seemed to remember there was something in his hand and he turned and placed it on the kitchen countertop, a thick slab of blond wood. "Julie brought us some wine." Turning to face Julie, he gestured. "Please, make yourself comfortable."

Julie chose a wooden rocking chair that had a woven seat cushion, like one of those miniature rugs of multi colors that her grandmother used to have in the house. The room was divided with a quilt that hung from the ceiling, a panel of blue and green pieces of fabric expertly stitched into a pattern that looked like sea glass against the sky. She assumed their bed was on the other side. The area was spotless, the air filled with the Christmasy scent of cinnamon and cloves. Sarah brought a yellow mug and set it on a table next to the rocking chair. She lowered herself to the floor.

"Oh! Did I take your chair?" Julie started to stand.

Sarah shook her head, smiling. "I enjoy sitting on the floor. Sometimes I sleep on the floor!" She crossed her legs in what Julie recognized from yoga class as the very difficult Lotus pose.

Well. Julie didn't know what to say about sleeping on the floor. Then again, Sarah looked to be about fourteen. And obviously very flexible.

Julie took a sip of tea. It was strong and bitter, and she imagined it might have been brewed from roots and twigs. "Thomas is in Arizona. I don't know if he told you."

"Oh yes, he told us. We were so sorry to see him go. But he needs to find his joy."

Zack nodded solemnly as he leaned against the wall.

"His joy," Julie repeated. "Yes. Well, he has responsibilities here, too. On the farm," she blurted.

Sarah clasped her hands in her lap and gazed at Julie. Her skirt was made out of an old pair of jeans, sewn together and covered with patches. She was lovely, Julie thought.

"I'm sorry," Julie said, with a glance up to Zack. She regretted the outburst. "I didn't mean to take any of my own frustrations out on you. It's just that this is our family's farm, and…"

"But it seems that no one else in the family is very interested in it," Zack pointed out, in a low, gentle voice that reminded Julie of how God would probably sound if he spoke to her. Zack could pick up on voiceovers when James Earl Jones was no longer able to speak.

Julie wrapped her fingers around the warm mug, and pretended to drink, taking the tiniest of sips. Maybe a little sugar would help, but it wasn't offered. Ugh. She lifted her chin and forced a big smile before rising.

"Thank you so much for the hospitality and the tea. I should get back to the house now. I need to make a few calls." She couldn't wait to talk to Freddy.

Sarah rose effortlessly from that impossible position and held her arms out. Julie allowed the embrace, even though she had more of an urge to pat Sarah's little head.

"You're always welcome here, Julie," Sarah said, taking Julie's hand and walking with her to the front door.

"Thanks. And, um, you're both always welcome at the main house, too," she said. She wondered if they regularly came to the house. And was that why Julie smelled apple pie yesterday? Maybe. She got in her car and waved to the couple standing on the front step, Zack who stood a foot and a half over Sarah.

THOMAS

Her name was Nikki. Of course it was. And Thomas didn't have to go through her purse to find it. Because once she started talking, she didn't stop.

"I have this friend Laura, right? So we were out last week and these guys from I don't know where just walked right up to us and asked us if we wanted to hook up! I was like, are you kidding me? And Laura said to me, she said, 'Nikki, no way in hell, right?' And I was like, 'Well, of course no way in hell!' Unreal, you know?"

Thomas's eyes had glazed over within the first five minutes. But at least he had her name.

"So, Thomas, when can I see you again?"

"Well, *Nikki*, I'm only out here for a visit. I have stuff to deal with at home, back east. I told you that last night."

She raised her palms to him. "Tell me you are not married. If I find out I've spent the night with another married man, I will freakin' kill myself."

"I'm not married, Nikki. But I'm not the man for you. Honest."

"So this was a one-night stand then?" She asked this question as she applied another coat of mascara to already-coated lashes.

"I'm afraid it was. Nikki. But we talked about all this last night. You said you wanted something casual." Thomas couldn't stop saying her name now that he had it.

She giggled. "I always say that. Hey, as long as I know. And thank you for being honest with me. If you want to see me one more time before you leave, call me." She picked up her purse, dug around for her car keys, and walked out of the pool house.

God, he didn't want to date.

Thomas showered, dressed, and crept into the kitchen, hoping to enjoy a cup of coffee without having to face Linda. But no. She was there, along with Don and Eric. They all turned to him, but only his brothers were grinning.

"Well, Tommy-boy, you couldn't even feed her breakfast before kicking her out of bed?" Eric lifted his coffee cup in salute.

"Shut up." He turned to Linda. "I apologize. I'm not a tequila drinker, obviously."

Linda lowered her eyes and filled his cup, then pushed it across the counter to him. "Not the girl for you?" She regarded him with those dark eyes. He couldn't tell what she was thinking, which was maybe just as well.

"She wasn't. And for the record, she wanted to keep things casual. I never led her on. But I'm willing to keep looking. Just without the benefit of tequila." He raised his coffee cup.

"Now that Christmas is behind us, tell me, Tom, what are your plans?" Don sat ramrod straight in his chair, years of military still evident in his posture. "You still think you want to live out here? And what does our Julie say about all of this?"

"Yeah, how is little Julie?" Eric asked, shoveling a forkful of scrambled eggs into his mouth.

"Julie's fine, Eric, not so little anymore. I mean, she's not fat, but she's all grown up. She's got a big job, nice place in New York City. She's up at the farm now." Thomas pulled apart a churro and popped a piece in his mouth, savoring the sweetness. Perfect balance to the strong coffee Linda served. "I can't sell the place without her. But I want to sell, so she'll need some convincing to let go of the property. And yes, Don, I want to live out here. I don't want to be a farmer anymore. Once the property is sold, I'll have enough money to get a little place and figure out what my next job will be."

"The end of the dairy farmer." Eric chuckled into his coffee and Thomas wanted to smack his fat face. Eric was a pain in the ass, but Thomas held his tongue. It wasn't his nature, and he didn't want to fight with his brother. His old, fat, balding brother.

"What is it you want to do, Tom?" Don pushed his plate to the side, and Linda picked it up immediately.

"You want eggs, Tommy?" Linda stood at the stove, ready to cook for him.

"Not right now, thanks. Donnie, I like being outside, especially in this climate. Maybe something at one of the golf courses, you know. I can fix things, keep the grounds maintained."

Don leaned back in his chair and considered. "All right, let me look into that. I know a few people."

"You want to come work for me in Austin? Lots of pretty girls there."

Thomas would no sooner work for Eric than bring Nikki back for a long conversation.

"I like it here in Arizona, Eric. But, thanks." He finished the churro and wiped his mouth.

"Suit yourself." Eric reached for two more strips of bacon from the nearly-depleted platter. He sat back on the barstool, his belly still pressed up against the counter. Draining the rest of his coffee and suppressing a burp behind his meaty hand, he said, "Great breakfast, Linda. Now, if you'll excuse me, I gotta hit the throne." He pushed back and grabbed the newspaper before heading upstairs.

Don shook his head. "What woman wouldn't want him?"

Linda rolled her eyes. "Men like that, as long as they're rich, will always have women. Not good women, but women." She turned to face Thomas. "You sure you don't want to eat, Tommy? Speak now or I'm going to clean up."

"Okay, okay. Two eggs, over easy, no bread." He patted his stomach. "Gotta stay trim for my future bride."

JULIE

Julie arrived back at the house and pulled off her boots. She flicked the switch to turn up the heat and hung her jacket on a wooden peg by the door. Oh, what the heck, she thought, I'm done for the day. Upstairs, in her bedroom, she slipped off her clothes and put on her favorite flannel pajamas, soft and worn. She changed into thick wool socks. Christmas was over for Julie this year. Moving on.

She dialed Freddy's number and waited. He picked up and she could hardly hear him with all the background noise. She shouted into the phone, "Freddy?"

He shouted back. "Hold on! I'm going into another room."

She heard a door shut and then only Freddy. "Better?"

"Yeah," she laughed. "Where are you?"

"In the bathroom upstairs. It's the only quiet room in the whole house right now. And I locked the door, too. Hey! Merry Christmas, sweetie!"

"Merry Christmas to you, too. How's your day been?"

"Not bad, actually. Loud and raucous, but I'm okay with it for one or two days. I may crash here tonight and take the train back in the morning. How are you?"

"I'm fine. My exciting day is over, and I'm back in my granny flannel pajamas."

"The ones with Curious George? Fetching. Farm life agrees with you."

"Har har. It was actually a nice day. The neighbors up the road are sweet, and I ate way too much, of course."

"Of course. Me, too."

"And then I went to see a young couple who live in the cottage at the edge of the property. Apparently Tommy hired them to do maintenance or something. Zack and Sarah. Freddy, they're like throwbacks to the sixties. True hippies, living off the land. Very nice, don't get me wrong."

Freddy began singing. "'Our house, is a very very very fine house'. So…Tommy never told you about them?"

"Of course not. But they seemed to know all about him. They weren't surprised he'd taken off, either. Maybe they're hoping he'll give them the farm."

"Well, don't get all worked up on Christmas night, doll. Are you coming back early?"

"Probably. There isn't any reason for me to stay. The farm is fine for now. Zack said the workers will be back in the morning. And I really need to nail down Tommy's plans." Julie pulled a blanket over her legs. She'd turned the heat up, but it was still freezing.

"So, are you willing to sell?"

"I don't know. I'm not sure I can. I just don't know what to do. I love this place, Freddy."

"Come back to the city tomorrow. I need some Julie time."

"Love you, babe."

"Good night, princess."

THOMAS

Don arranged for Thomas to meet with the manager of the Painted Desert Country Club on Saturday. Linda helped him to craft a decent resume and printed out a few copies for him.

Thomas dressed in gray slacks, a white Oxford shirt, and a casual navy blazer. He knew he was overdressed for a job at the golf course but wanted to present a professional look. Don drove him to the business office and Thomas waited to meet with the manager while Don hit a bucket of balls on the driving range.

He didn't have a turf degree, and the manager informed him that if another candidate had the right education, he or she would be chosen over Thomas, but based on his brother's recommendation, the job was his if he wanted it. The pay was fair, and Thomas figured he could always pick up extra work here and there. And benefits! He'd have benefits after his probation period. Now he could ask Don and Linda if he could live in the guest house until he found an apartment. But first, he'd need to fly home and convince Julie to let him put the farm up for sale.

"This calls for a celebration," Linda said when the men arrived back home. "No tequila though, right?" She winked at Thomas.

"No tequila. Maybe a beer."

"So, the job is yours," Don said, nodding with satisfaction.

"Well, unless someone with a degree in turf management applies within the next week or two."

"That's not likely."

"No, guess not." Thomas accepted the cold can from Linda and popped the top. Arizona Wilderness was a local brewery, and they made some damn good beer. He set the can on a woven placement and looked at Don.

"I need to get everything in order. I'm gonna fly back to talk with Julie. I know she's not happy with the idea of selling, but I can guarantee she doesn't want to run a dairy farm, and when I let her know what it's worth, I think she'll go along. It's just not a conversation I can have over the phone. It wouldn't be fair to her. And I can tie up some loose ends while I'm in Dalton."

"When would you start the new job?

"Next month, Phil said. The guy they got now is retiring at the end of January, so he'd want me on for at least a week with him. I've got time, but I need to book a flight home today." Home, Thomas thought, would have a completely different meaning soon.

"Use the laptop in the den," Linda said. "We're taking you out for dinner tonight."

"The three of us?" He cocked an eyebrow at his sister-in-law, hoping she'd pick up on his question.

"No, there'll be four, okay? We're going to try this again. My cousin's friend Maria is twenty-nine and single. She teaches second grade. And she's gorgeous. And she's *not* a casual hook-up."

"I'm in!" Thomas headed into the den to book a flight home. He'd sit down with his sister and they'd figure out what to do with the farm. And as soon as they did, he'd fly back. Maybe Zack would buy his truck.

JULIE

Julie spent Friday walking around the village. She never ran into Zack or Sarah, although Zack in the far distance raised his arm in greeting. She waved back, but kept walking. He had work to do on the property, and she'd decided this would be her last day in Dalton. She'd travel back on Saturday rather than Sunday, and probably would manage to avoid some of the crowds as well. The roast had thawed, so she put it in the oven and added onions, carrots, and potatoes. It was too much food for just her, but she couldn't decide whether to ask Zack and Sarah over for dinner (what would they talk about?) or mention it to Ethan and Pauline, who couldn't bring the kids because there wasn't enough food, and it looked as though they still had house guests. So, it would be Zack and Sarah. Of course, she could always just eat her share alone and swing by the cottage with the leftovers. But that wasn't the way her parents would have acted. Julie could hear her mother's voice. "There's always room for another at our table."

She checked the little book next to the old black push-button phone in the hallway. Did Ethan mention Zack's last name? No. She started at the beginning and thumbed through the entries, all written in Thomas's scrawl. Andy. Abe's Hardware. Barber. Dentist. Julie rolled her eyes and flipped to the back of the little book. There. Zack/Sarah. She picked up the phone and dialed.

"Greetings," Sarah's little-girl voice chirped.

"Sarah, hi. It's Julie Tate."

"Hello, Julie. Nice to hear from you."

"Yes, same here. Listen, Sarah, I'm cooking a roast that Tommy left for me. It's way too much food for just me to eat, and I'm leaving here tomorrow morning. Would you and Zack like to join me for dinner? That is, if you haven't already planned something." They ate meat, right? Julie wasn't sure.

"No, Julie, we don't have anything planned, and that sounds lovely. What time should we arrive?" Her voice was as light as mist.

Julie glanced at the clock on the stove. "Is five okay? Will Zack be finished with his work by then?" She was hoping for an early night.

Sarah laughed softly. "Zack is never finished! But yes, five is fine. I made bread today. Why don't I bring it?"

"Fabulous." Bread. Carbs. "See you then, Sarah." She disconnected the call and headed upstairs to take a long, hot shower.

THOMAS

Dinner at Binkley's was top-notch, one of the best meals Thomas had ever eaten. He'd had to wear a necktie, but when he saw Maria, he knew it was worth the discomfort around his neck. She was gorgeous, just as Linda had promised. He guessed she was part or all Mexican, and in that red dress, he couldn't stop staring. He silently thanked his father for teaching him how to behave properly.

Don ordered steak tartare and frogs' legs for the table, and Thomas kept his mouth shut; after all, Don chose the restaurant, and made a point of telling Thomas earlier that he'd foot the bill. But raw meat and frogs' legs? Thomas sipped the wine Don selected from a separate menu as well, foregoing his usual beer. He was grateful that a young man, whose only job was to refill water glasses, stayed close and attentive.

Thomas's ribeye cost forty-seven dollars. The baked potato was five bucks. He knew he wouldn't be coming to this place again, not with a job as assistant groundskeeper. He hoped Maria wasn't the kind of woman who expected to be taken to fancy places. The more he thought about it, the madder he got. Don was setting him up, and every place he took Maria to after tonight would be a letdown. Unless he explained. He'd have to tell her the truth and hope she wouldn't walk away. Even though she'd look damn good walking away.

After dinner, they returned to Don and Linda's palace. Again it struck Thomas that perhaps Maria would expect him to live in a similar house. He leaned in close and whispered in her ear, "You know, my brother lives a different life than I do." She turned her pretty face to him and grinned wide, a sparkling white smile that seemed as if it was lit from within. She didn't lean away, and whispered back to him.

"Thomas, I teach second grade. I've never been to a restaurant like that."

He gripped her hand and squeezed.

JULIE

Zack and Sarah were wonderful dinner companions, Julie had to admit. She set aside any judgments and simply enjoyed their company. They had amazing tales to tell, how they met as high school students in California, traveled for a year to Malawi to work with underprivileged children, and how they found Jingle Valley and the cottage after traveling to Stockbridge to see the original Alice's Restaurant.

"Alice's Restaurant!" Julie exclaimed. "How did you even know about that place?"

"My parents used to sing it when I was little," Sarah said, her eyes drifting away from the table to a place in the past. "My grandpa knew Arlo Guthrie."

"I'm going back to the city tomorrow morning. I don't know when Tommy is coming back, but I just want to thank you both for keeping an eye on everything." She spoke directly to Zack. "It means a lot to know the farm is in good hands."

Zack dipped his head in appreciation. "No problem, not at all," he said. He lifted his eyes to hers and paused. "Did Thomas tell you he's coming back?"

"Um, well, he was vague," Julie said. "I know he needed a break…" She trailed off, unsure what to say. They must know, since Sarah said they were sorry to see him go. This would be a good time to end the evening. "Anyway, thanks again, for everything. And for the delicious bread, Sarah." Three slices of that bread, with honey butter, had done her in. She pushed back from the table.

After Zack and Sarah had left, taking with them whatever food remained from the meal, Julie cleaned the kitchen thoroughly, leaving it as she'd found it. She composed a long letter to Tommy, in which she stated how much she loved the farm, and hoped they could talk about it very soon. She folded the letter, slid it into a plain white envelope she found in his desk, and wrote his name on the front, then stood the envelope up against the brass candlesticks that had belonged to her grandmother.

She fell asleep easily that night, knowing that she'd made her position clear.

THOMAS

Thomas took Maria by the hand and led her to the pool house, but only so he could kiss her in private. And man, was it nice to kiss her! Her lips were soft and yielding, and her hair smelled like tropical fruit, coconut and pineapple. He pictured the two of them on an island, or down in Mexico, soaking up the sun. She'd be glistening and brown, and he'd be slathered in zinc oxide so his fair Norwegian skin wouldn't turn lobster-red. Lovely. He traced his finger down her bare arm.

"I wish we could go swimming," he said in a low voice.

"I didn't bring my bathing suit," she whispered.

"I know."

With a soft smile, she drew back, then kissed him full on the mouth again. "I had a nice time tonight. So, you're flying back home tomorrow?" Maria stood and stepped to the window, where she gazed out at the pool, shimmering silvery-blue in the moonlight.

"Yeah. Just to settle a few things with my sister." He met her eyes when she turned to him. "I'll be back as soon as I can. Can I see you again?" He moved to her and held onto her hand, pressing his lips to her palm. He liked that he had some height on her.

"Of course," she said, lowering her thick black lashes before tilting her chin to look up at him. "Hurry back," she added before breaking into a grin.

Thomas exhaled. He felt as eager-hearted as a boy in summer.

JULIE

By the time Julie had closed up the house, replaced the key, packed up her rental car and brought it back to the drop-off station in Albany, she barely had enough time to grab a cup of coffee before boarding her train.

The ride back to Manhattan seemed to take forever, but it provided an opportunity for Julie to think things through. How would the conversation with Tommy go? She didn't want to fight with him, and she needed to have a plan to counter with if he was adamant about selling. She sent a text to Freddy:

Arrival sched 10:26. You up?

She set the phone on her thigh and stared out the window. In a minute or so, she had a reply:

Be @ train sta

She smiled. Freddy was her best friend. Her girlfriends were great, and she missed spending time with them, but motherhood and marriage had sucked away any free time they used to have, when they'd go out for drinks, see movies, walk around Greenwich Village. And if she were being honest, Julie really didn't care for an afternoon with her friends that was dominated by hours at the playground, listening to other young mothers complain about the nanny, the pre-school, the husband. She felt as though she had nothing in common with them anymore.

She exited the train and stepped onto the escalator, holding her bag by the handles, always mindful of who was around her. She was a smart city girl. So when someone jostled her on her left just as she stepped on solid ground, she immediately felt in her pockets. You could never be too safe around Penn Station.

"Jules!" Freddy screamed, oblivious to the stares from people near him. She flung herself into his embrace and kissed him on both cheeks.

"How's my little farm girl?" Freddy wore a beige beret, and looked positively French with his little goatee and black glasses. Of course, no one in France wears a beret these days; only Freddy could pull it off and look chic.

"You're so sweet to meet me. I've only had coffee. Can we eat?"

"Of course we can eat! It's the holidays. Let's eat big. Big bagels and oily lox." He wrapped his arm around her waist and led her toward the street.

"I can't eat big. I have to fit into my dress for New Year's Eve."

"Honey, you look fabulous. He'll think so, too. Have lox and eggs. Come on."

"You can eat anything," Julie muttered as she let Freddy take her bag.

They exited the station and Freddy lifted his arm to hail a cab. As soon as one pulled up, they slid into the back seat and Freddy directed the driver. The cab stopped in front of The Grey Dog and they hopped out. Most of Manhattan was still asleep on this Sunday after Christmas and the place was nearly empty.

Over smoked salmon toast points with a side of bacon, Freddy regaled Julie with tales of his family's antics. Julie talked about the farm, about Ethan and Pauline, and Zack and Sarah. She was still talking when Freddy held up his hand.

"What?" She used a knife to push the last bits of egg onto her fork.

"Hear me out on this. I've been dying to tell you."

Julie slid her plate to the side and waited.

"Okay, so Tommy wants to sell the farm, right? And you want to *keep* the farm."

"Yes. But I can't run a dairy farm. Zack and Sarah are sweet kids, but I don't think they're up to running it, either. The guys who come to milk the cows and feed the chickens? They're contract workers. Once they finish up at Jingle Valley, they move on." She accepted a refill of coffee.

"Jules, you've been saying for the past year that you're burned out at work."

She hadn't even mentioned the email from Barton Thayer, but he was right. She was burned out, and now also concerned about possible layoffs. "Yep."

Freddy took an exaggerated breath before speaking. "Okay, here it is. You buy Tommy out, not all at once, but like a mortgage. You keep the farm, but sell off all the cows and chickens and whatever other farm animals you have running around up there. And you turn it into a resort. A bed and breakfast. A destination wedding place!" He clapped his hands. Julie stared at him.

"That's your idea?"

"Yes. Doll! It would be fabulous. And here's the best part: I'd go into business with you. We could do this! The house isn't shabby or anything, is it?"

"No, but it would need work." Julie tried to concentrate, but Freddy was so animated, and talking so fast, she could only sit and listen and answer his questions.

"How many bedrooms? Bathrooms?" He bounced in his chair.

"There's a master bedroom downstairs, with a bathroom attached. Um, five bedrooms upstairs, two bathrooms. But Freddy, wait. I'm still trying to wrap my head around all of this."

"Jules, it could work! We could even convert the barn. Wait! It's coming to me now," he said, staring off into space as if possessed by the Great Idea God. He held up his hands, like a sculptor, and forming an idea, a plan, out of the air in front of them. "We convert the barn – that will be the wedding venue. Add a honeymoon suite onto it." He put his hand out and used it to push her chin up, closing her gaping mouth.

"Oh my God," Julie whispered.

"It's a great idea! It's not that far by train, it's a hell of a lot cheaper than anything here in the city, and it's cool! Everyone's into this farm to table movement," he said, waving his hands in the air. True enough, even the restaurant they were in was all about locally-sourced food.

"It would need so much work. I don't know." Julie shook her head and exhaled.

"It's an opportunity. You can be your own boss. And those hippies? Keep them! He fixes stuff, right? She cooks, right?"

"Yeah."

"Okay. Look, we could convert the house to a B&B – I could do it - but I really think your money is going to be in booking weddings there. And," he added, pointing a long finger at her face, "it's something you can tell Tommy."

Something she could tell Tommy. Yes. She thought about that for a minute while Freddy, looking very pleased with himself, lifted his Bloody Mary in a solo toast and drank.

"Weddings. In the barn. And you'd be in on this with me? You'd move to Dalton?"

Her friend lifted his broad shoulders and turned his palms upward. "I will. I'll do it, Julie. I'll be a gay farm boy."

She couldn't help but laugh. And suddenly she felt lighter, in spite of having just eaten everything on her plate.

THOMAS

Thomas's plane touched down Sunday afternoon and he rented a car to drive back to Dalton. He regretted not leaving his truck at the airport, but was just glad to get back to the farm before Julie left on Monday. He'd surprise her, but they'd have time to talk this thing through, at least. The sooner he could convince her to sell, the sooner he could begin his new life. Meeting Maria had inspired him to move quickly.

He knew the drive from Albany, and kept to the speed limit, knowing where the cops hid. By the time he turned onto the road that led down to Jingle Valley, it was almost six and dark. One dim light was on in the kitchen, but Tommy didn't see a car. Julie would have a car. He pulled in next to his truck, reminding himself to drive it tomorrow, and let himself into the house.

"Julie!" he called to the darkness. It was chilly inside. He checked the thermostat. Down to sixty degrees. She must be freezing; was she afraid to turn up the heat? "Jules! It's Tommy!" His voice echoed in the stillness. What the hell?

He pulled out his phone, but it needed to be charged, and he didn't have the energy to dig for his charger in his bag. He opened the little book next to the land phone and looked up her number. He picked up the old black phone and dialed her cell, never seeing the white envelope propped up in front of the candlesticks on the shelf above the stove.

JULIE

Julie set her alarm for six. The idea of quitting her job and moving to Jingle Valley, with Freddy, gave her a nauseating wave of nervousness, coupled with a tingle of excitement. Tomorrow she'd stop in to see Axel before work and confirm their plans for New Year's Eve. If she was serious about relocating, then Axel was indeed a casual thing, and maybe that's all she needed right now.

It's not as if the idea hadn't crossed her mind before. Manhattan could be exhausting at times, and when she dreamed of living somewhere else, an image of Jingle Valley was always first to come to mind. Freddy had pushed a button, one that inspired her to take a giant leap of trust and faith that leaving PCM, leaving New York, could be the right decision.

She and Freddy had talked all day, hashing out plans, considering as many options as they could. Both of them had available money to put into the venture, enough to get them six months into the project, at least. Harmony had mentioned a friend who was looking to move to the city; maybe she'd take the apartment.

Her cell phone rang and she saw that it was Tommy calling. She took a deep breath and readied herself for the conversation.

"Hey, Tommy."

"Why aren't you here at the farm?"

"Uh, hey. I'm fine, thanks for asking. And Merry Christmas. What do you mean, *here* at the farm?"

"I flew back to see you. To talk with you in person." He was ticked off, Julie could tell. She smiled at the thought.

"I took the train back this morning."

Thomas chuckled harshly. "Couldn't stand it, could you? I know you, Julie."

"I don't think you do. You still want to sell the farm?"

"Yep." Tense reply. He was gearing up for a fight, Julie could tell.

"Good."

"What? You're okay with this now?"

"I am. Because you're going to sell it to me. I'm buying you out."

"Huh? Come on, Jules, quit kidding. I'm exhausted from the flight."

"Well then, sit down, put your feet up, and listen. I am buying you out of your half. Jingle Valley is staying in the Tate family for as long as I can help it."

"You don't know the first thing about running a dairy farm."

"You're right." She willed herself to be calm, to keep her voice even. Tommy would not get the fight he seemed to want so badly.

"So, is this going to be like an investment? Like, you own it and hire a team to run it while you do your executive thing in New York?"

"No, Tommy. I'm going to live there. In the house. I'll let Zack and Sarah stay in the cottage; they're lovely and very helpful." She could hear her brother mouth-breathing on the other end. "There's a lot of potential for the barn, maybe a place for parties, weddings." She held her breath, waiting for his reaction.

"You're nuts, you know that? You're gonna get in way over your head with this, and all because of sentimentality. Because of the past. The past is gone, Julie. Why can't you let it go?"

Julie counted silently to five before responding. "Listen to me. You want out. I want to keep the place. Whatever needs to be done for me to buy out your share, I'll do it."

She heard his boots on the hardwood floor of the living room. He should have taken off his boots before walking on that floor, she thought. Finally he spoke.

"You have any idea what this place is worth?"

"I have a pretty good idea." She quoted him a figure, her best guess.

He let out a low whistle. "You're good, Jules. That's pretty close to what the appraiser told me last month."

"So let's get a lawyer and get this thing done. Then you can get back to sunny Phoenix." She paused and softened her tone. "So, how is it out there? Do you really like it?"

His voice softened as well, and he was her brother again, not someone with whom she was doing a business deal. "It's paradise, Jules. Gorgeous. Don and Linda have been letting me stay in their guest house. And I met a girl, a woman. She's a schoolteacher. She's pretty and sweet and I like her a lot. There's something about the area. I just feel like I belong there. I know it must sound crazy to you."

It did sound crazy. She'd been to Phoenix once, to visit Don and Linda, back before she'd risen in the firm and had little free time. Phoenix was dry and hot and brown. Yes, her brother had a beautiful home and a sparkling aquamarine pool. They'd done very well for themselves, and she was proud of him. But she couldn't imagine ever living in the southwest, in the desert. All of her siblings had left the Berkshire Mountains far behind and moved west. But this was Tommy's choice, not hers. She just hoped it wasn't one of those instances where you go on vacation, and everything is so relaxed and nice that you think you want to move there permanently. She knew that feeling.

Taking a breath, she spoke. "I'm glad, Tommy. Really. So let's see if we can get this thing done, okay? The sooner the better."

"I agree. I'll call Bob Gleason in the morning. He's always handled the legal issues for me."

"Okay. Let me know." She disconnected and set the phone down. Outside her window, the city was bright. She peered down to the street, where red taillights in a line stretched as far as she could see. Traffic, even on Sunday evening of a holiday weekend. The city that never sleeps. Moving back to Dalton would be a big adjustment, for her and also, especially, for Freddy. But he'd been so excited about the plans for the farm, and

Julie had to admit, a change would be good. She could leave PCM before it went under, if that was the future for her employer. Turn Jingle Valley into a wedding destination? Could they do it? She'd been the party planner for her family and friends. She had an MBA, for Pete's sake, of course she could run a business. Besides, she had faith in Freddy. He could do anything. Together they'd make it happen.

***

CoffeeX was open early on Monday morning. Julie pushed on the door and walked into warm air filled with the scent of cinnamon. Axel wasn't behind the counter; he must be in the kitchen, Julie thought, picturing his long fingers, pliant and probing, working the dough. She shook her head to dispel the image.

"Help you?" It was the girl from the other day. Her face didn't register any hint of recognition. Actually, she looked hungover. Maybe she was.

"Nonfat latte, large." She eyed the pastries lining the display window and her stomach grumbled in reply. She turned her gaze to the counter and picked up a yellow banana. Step away from the carbs, she thought. "And this, too."

The girl turned to make her coffee.

"Is Axel here?" Julie tried to sound casual, like it didn't matter one way or the other.

"He'll be in later," the girl said, placing the cup in front of Julie. "So, the coffee and the banana?"

"That's it," Julie said. Damn it. She'd text him from the office, maybe make a return trip at lunch. She handed over some money to the girl and dropped coins into the tip jar. This girl wasn't very friendly. But as soon as Julie had passed silent judgment against the girl, she forgave her. Poor thing – who'd want to be in here on a cold Monday morning. Julie threw an extra dollar into the jar but the girl didn't acknowledge it.

***

She was practically alone in her office. Harmony was off this week – it was school vacation. Most of the younger workers, the ones with small children, took time off between Christmas and New Year's. Anyone below manager level wouldn't have received the email that Barton had sent, and Julie wondered when layoff notices would go out. Some firms let employees go just before Christmas – about the Grinchiest thing anyone could do. PCM probably figured they'd get the year-end business from everyone and lower the boom in January.

Julie sipped her coffee and opened a document on her computer. She knew how to draft a resignation letter, but her fingers wouldn't work this morning. Cold feet? Nah, she told herself, this was the right thing to do. She just wished someone would affirm her decision for her, someone other than Freddy. Was she being impulsive? Very much so. Crazy? Possibly. But was their plan doable? Julie paused. Yes. It was doable. They could do this. And Freddy's idea about making the farm a destination wedding venue was just nutty enough to work. If anyone could make this happen, it's us, Julie thought. He had as much drive and determination as she did, and he was skilled at carpentry and renovation. Seven years earlier, she'd asked a friend at work for a recommendation – her bathroom needed a makeover, and her co-worker had offered Freddy's number. They'd met for coffee and worked out all the particulars, and he'd been in her apartment for weeks. He put in a new toilet, added new tile around the shower, put in a recessed medicine cabinet, and painted everything bright white. She'd had no idea he was gay, until she embarrassed herself by making a silly move at the end of the day, a move he'd gallantly and gently deflected.

It was too early to rouse her new business partner. He enjoyed sleeping in, as he called it, although that would have to change once they started working together. Jingle Valley Weddings? Weddings at Jingle Valley? She was adamant about the name - no way would it be called anything other than Jingle Valley, and Freddy was fine with that.

And what about Axel? There was chemistry between them, she was sure of it, but now she'd made a decision to leave. Leave the city, her apartment, and any chance of the two of them being more than flirty acquaintances. Casual hook-ups were never her thing, and even with all the life-changing decisions she'd made recently, she wasn't about to do something stupid. He was cute, he made her feel pretty, and she wasn't averse to dancing with him on New Year's Eve. That would have to do.

Time passed as she attempted to complete some work, but with the six or so people in the office who were also on holiday mode, nothing much was accomplished. At ten-thirty, she called Freddy. And woke him up.

"Julie, what are you doing? It's too early." His voice was muddled with sleep.

"Sorry. Really. But, you know, you can't be sleeping in once we're running this business."

"We're not running the business yet. I'm going back to sleep." He hung up on her.

Julie rested her chin on her hand. Should she write the resignation letter now? Yes.

She typed out the draft in no time, but knew it needed work. It had to be good. And appreciative. She checked her boss's schedule online. He was on vacation all this week, not returning until January 5. Ugh. Julie knew she'd have to speak with him. She saved the document and just before she closed the file, added a password and changed the name of the document to TemplateRL.

She stared at her cell phone, again. Scrolling, she found Axel's number in her contacts list and composed a message.

Missed you this morning! Nope. Erase. Hi! Looked for you this morning. Erase. Hope to catch up with you today. Let me know when you're in. Fine. Whatever. She hit send.

So now I'm waiting on four men, Julie thought. Axel. Tommy. Freddy. And Maxwell, her boss. Four men had to respond to her in order for her life to move forward. Julie sighed. Isn't that always the way?

She heard back from Axel first. He's not busy either, she thought, turning away from real work to focus on his message.

I'm here! Come in for lunch. I made soup xx

Well. He liked using the xx at the end, but maybe that was just habit on his part. Harmony did it, too, only with one x.

She'd stop in before lunch and pick up some soup. Of course, there was no way of knowing if she'd run into Christopher again, although he probably had the week off for precious family time. Applewhite Skipworth's offices were steps away from CoffeeX. What would Christopher think of her new venture? He'd think she was crazy, although she recalled he loved the farm that time she brought him up to meet Tommy. It surprised her at the time that he was so comfortable there, but only served to endear him to her more.

Well, she'd likely not see Christopher again. As it should be, she told herself. Looking backward had always been her problem. And if she was honest, it's probably what had her so set on buying Jingle Valley, too.

Was it lunchtime yet?

Freddy called an hour later. "Good morning!" he chirped. She glanced at the clock on her wall.

"Just barely," she muttered. "You know, you need to start adjusting to early mornings. There's a lot you can accomplish before noon."

"Mm-mm. Hold on while I finish this bagel."

"I'm going to start getting you up by eight. You can't sleep away the morning!"

"Chill, doll. I'll be up and at 'em every morning. I mean, what kind of nightlife exists in Dalton? We'll be in bed at sunset, right?"

"Very funny." She relayed the conversation she'd had with Thomas.

"Did you tell him about me?"

"Not in that conversation. I figured it would be better to ease him into it."

"Hmm. And how did he take it?"

"Okay, I guess. He's contacting his lawyer today. We'll figure things out. I know he wants to finalize everything so he can get back to Arizona. Apparently he's already met someone. How come it's so easy for him?"

"Your brother's a hottie." When she didn't respond, he added, "You are, too. Coffee boy thinks so."

"Don't call him that." She stood up and closed her office door. "Listen, I'm drafting my resignation letter this morning." She still hadn't told him anything about the email from Barton Thayer or what she feared was the possible demise of Provident Capital Management.

She heard Freddy draw water from a faucet.

"I've pretty much written the letter, but Maxwell's off this week for a family vacation in Aspen. I need to get in touch with him; this thing can't be done by email, or by phone. I just want everything ready for him when he comes back to work. And if I can't reach him, I'll end up springing it on him the day he returns."

"Honey, it's not your fault. Stop worrying about him. Now, something tells me you're itching to get out of the office and walk down the street to see your hot lunch date. I'll talk to you later."

Julie checked her hair and makeup, then headed out without a coat.

***

The girl from the morning was leaving just as Julie opened the door to CoffeeX.

"Hi again!" she said to the girl, giving her a bright smile.

"You're so obvious," the girl muttered before pushing past her and out into the cold day.

Julie looked behind her, startled at the girl's observation. Was she that obvious? That wasn't her style, to chase after men. Perhaps she should stay away from CoffeeX this week. She didn't want to get stupid about a New Year's Eve date.

The shop was quiet, and Axel was alone, apparently letting his young employee go home to sleep away the afternoon.

"Julie!" He stepped from behind the counter and looked down at his hands. The palms were white, covered with flour. He wiped them on his apron. "How pretty you look today," he murmured.

"It's quiet this week. Everyone's off."

"Except us. We keep working," he said with a smile. "So you came in for my soup?" He turned back to the service area behind the counter.

Thoughts filled Julie's head – an empty coffee shop, icing, sugar, probably a serviceable table in the back. "Yes, soup," she said. "To go, please." She should get back to the office.

He gestured to two empty café tables in front of the plate-glass window. "You're welcome to stay, you know."

"Maybe a few minutes."

"Do you want coffee? Something cold instead?" Julie shook her head and sat on one of the tiny chairs that was far too lightweight to be real wrought iron.

It was all so very sweet, so charmed, this back-and-forth between them. Raging fantasies in Julie's head were filtered by reason. She would be leaving the city soon. This was silly.

"Um, Axel. About New Year's Eve…"

He carried a bowl of soup on a tray and set it on the equally-tiny table. He'd added a napkin, spoon, and good-sized chunk of baguette.

"You want to change your mind?" With a glance to the door, he lowered himself to the other chair and searched her eyes.

"I'm leaving soon. I'm resigning from my job and moving to Massachusetts. I didn't want to give you the impression that I thought this would be something…"

He sat back and grinned. "Try the soup, please." He waited as she dipped her spoon and brought the creamy orange concoction to her lips. "Well?"

She closed her eyes. It was wonderful. "It's great. Sweet potato?"

Axel nodded. "Roasted sweet potato soup, my mother's recipe." He watched Julie take another spoonful. "Julie, there's no reason we can't go to a New Year's Eve party together. I'm not looking for a relationship, okay? I already have a girlfriend. Hey, are you okay? You sure? Take a sip of water, there. Good. Anyway, she's in Barcelona for six months doing research, and we're very open about being able to date, but, like I said, I wouldn't be looking for anything permanent. So why don't we go to this party?"

All Julie could do was nod and shovel roasted sweet potato soup, his mother's recipe, into her mouth as quickly as possible.

***

Maxwell's cell phone was never turned off. He was that kind of boss, much to his wife's chagrin. Julie had met Madeleine Koffrow a few times at work functions, and knew Madeleine was frustrated with her husband's inability to unplug. That was why Julie hesitated to call or text him. It wasn't so much that she was afraid to speak to him, but knowing that his wife would be upset kept her from dialing his number.

She debated texting or doing nothing. Springing her resignation on Maxwell on Monday seemed callous and unprofessional. Calling him to tell him about her plans was wrong, too. But she knew her boss, and knew he did not like surprises.

Instead of calling, she sent a text. *All fine @ work. If you have a minute tho, would like to speak w you.* She hoped he'd understand that there was no emergency at the office. He could call her at his leisure. He'd probably assume it was about the email from Barton.

Tommy hadn't phoned, and Julie wondered if he was able to get in touch with the lawyer. It was in the best interest of everyone for Tommy to find him and start the process, but she'd wait until tomorrow to call him. This afternoon, she tried to focus on work and year-end reports. When she did finally speak with Maxwell, she didn't want any of her business left undone. She would leave with her head held high, proud of the work she'd done for the company these past nine years.

"Nine years," Julie murmured. This was her first big job out of graduate school, and PCM was in many respects her family. It wasn't an easy decision to leave, although the email from Barton had given her a nudge. Get out ahead of the fall, she thought. Her father's brother Neal had been a banker in the eighties, when banks rose and fell like the tide. He'd always managed to leave one bank just before it collapsed or was merged into a bigger bank. Julie would emulate her Uncle Neal, and leave PCM before it was gobbled up by one of the giants.

THOMAS

Thomas entered the offices of Robert K. Gleason & Associates in Pittsfield and took a seat in the front foyer. He appreciated that Bob Gleason had made time to meet him today, after Thomas impressed upon him the nature of the meeting and the fact that he wanted to fly back to Phoenix as soon as possible.

He had put on a corduroy blazer, and a fresh white shirt, but he couldn't stop his right leg from bouncing up and down as he waited. Bob must have heard him come in, as he appeared in the doorway within a minute or two. The front desk, where his assistant usually sat, was empty. Just as well, Thomas thought – he couldn't remember her name.

"Happy holidays, Tom! Great to see you again."

"Thanks for seeing me today, Bob. I appreciate it." Thomas followed him down a short corridor to his office. He was well aware that Bob Gleason was the only attorney in the firm, but even sole practitioners used the 'and Associates' add-on. He had a spacious office with large windows on two walls, and Thomas looked out at a picturesque view of the Berkshires in winter. They really were dreamlike, Thomas thought. If someone had to sit in an office all day, at least there was a good view here, he thought.

"So, you're looking to sell Jingle Valley, and your sister Julie wants to buy you out," Bob said.

"Yeah. We own it half and half, but I'm looking to move to the southwest. I have a brother who lives there, and I just flew back in to get this process going. Julie surprised me when she said she wanted it, but it's been in our family for generations, and she's pretty sentimental that way." He shrugged, and wished he wasn't wearing the jacket, which was too tight through the shoulders.

"My father worked for your grandfather, Tom, back when he was a teen. It's a great place, Jingle Valley. I can understand why Julie wants to hang onto it." He peered over his glasses at Thomas, who shifted in his chair.

"Sure. I get that, too. Anyway, she's got some crazy plans for the barn, after she does some renovations, of course. You know, it's her call." He shook his head, remembering their conversation. "I just think she's out of her mind, but you know, whatever."

Bob Gleason cleared his throat. "Do you have the appraisal from last year with you?"

Thomas nodded and pulled it from a leather folder he'd brought with him. He handed it to Bob, who looked it over.

"Okay. This probably hasn't changed much. Real estate prices have pretty much stabilized, so the value looks to be fair. And Julie, is she going to buy you out directly or mortgage the property?"

"A mortgage, I think. We just want to know that we can move ahead with this."

"I don't see why not. You can't sell without her approval, and she gives approval by purchasing the farm. I can draw up the paperwork this week. Terry's on vacation until after New Year's, but it shouldn't be a problem."

Terry! That's her name. "I'm heading back to Arizona," Thomas said. "Do I need to stick around? Or will I need to come back?"

"Probably not," Bob said. "We can FedEx all the papers to you. This is completely amicable, right?"

"Oh yeah, Julie's fine with it."

Bob nodded. He leaned back in his big leather chair and rocked slightly. "I'll miss you, Tom. Wish you all the best. For the life of me, I can't imagine living anywhere but here, but I know a lot of folks head west for the climate. Good luck to you." He stood and held out his hand.

Thomas grasped it and shook. "Thanks. It's the right place for me. Come out for a visit sometime."

Bob Gleason took off his glasses and rubbed his eyes. "Sure. Have a good flight back."

***

Thomas arrived back in Phoenix and telephoned Maria from the airport.

"I hope it's not too late," he said when she picked up.

"Almost," she replied, her voice warm and silken. "A teacher's day starts early, even on school vacation. There's a lot of planning to do for the next semester."

Thomas glanced at his watch. It was only nine o'clock. "Sorry, I just wanted you to know that I'm back, and I missed you."

"You're sweet," she said. There was a moment of silence until Thomas spoke.

"Do you think we could see each other on New Year's Eve? That is, if you're free."

"Sure, I'd like to see you, too. What did you have in mind?"

Thomas closed his eyes and imagined. "Dinner and a movie? Or is that too boring?"

She laughed and it sounded like music. "That's fine. But let me cook for you. All the restaurants will be booked. And we can watch something at home. I'd rather be comfortable. Want to come to my place at seven?"

"Sounds good. See you then."

He would start looking for his own apartment next week.

JULIE

It was New Year's Eve day and Julie had stopped in the office to run a few reports. PCM was closed until Monday, and being alone on the floor was disconcerting. Maxwell still hadn't called, but her phone was on in case he tried to reach her. After three hours on the noiseless floor, she'd had enough. Outside on the sidewalk, it took ten minutes to hail a cab, but the taxi was preferable to the deserted subway.

Back in her apartment, she took a quick shower, dried her hair, and stood naked in front of her closet.

"I have no clothes!" she wailed to the crammed-full closet. She called Freddy.

"What are you wearing?" she asked.

"Now? Not a blessed thing, sugar."

"No, to the party tonight. What should I wear? And why didn't I figure this out before now?"

"Go with 'creative cocktail.' For me, black flannel trousers and my velvet blazer. I'm trying to impress. You should wear that gorgeous bronze sheath – you know the one I like? With lots of gold. What do you have for shoes?"

"Ugh, it's freezing out. And my legs are so white."

"Honey! You'll be in a cab or inside, we're not going for a stroll. Okay, what about the dove-gray maxi-dress with your red boots?"

"You should be here in my closet right now."

"Take that back."

"Freddy! Okay, the maxi-dress and the boots. Thank you."

"Is Coffee Boy picking you up?"

"Uh, no. I gave him your friends' address and told him I'd meet him there. *You're* picking me up." She heard him chuckle on the other end but said nothing. She'd bet money that Freddy would meet someone at the party. Axel's Barcelona-bound girlfriend had thrown a bucket of ice water, from thirty-eight hundred miles away, on whatever schoolgirl fantasy Julie had created in her mind about the two of them.

"I'll be there at nine."

***

The next morning, Julie woke at five, feeling as if she'd been hit head-on by an eighteen-wheeler. Her self-imposed promise not to drink evaporated when Axel never showed. Four (five?) glasses of champagne, deep-fried lobster, and some kind of creamy crab dip fought with each other all night, until they all surrendered and announced their hasty departure at three in the morning. Her stomach was devoid of contents, and the thought of coffee nauseated her. So did the thought of Coffee Boy, that rat. Maybe the girlfriend flew in to surprise him. Whatever. After learning of her existence, Julie had to admit the tingling had dissipated. Besides, she had big plans. Getting out of bed wasn't one of them.

And Freddy did meet a guy at the party. Julie should have figured as much; his options were seemingly unlimited. Gorgeous, hunky gay guys. While she ingested food and drink that wouldn't stay in her stomach (where they belonged), Freddy hit it off with an older man who had no fashion sense (Freddy must have seen it as a project, she surmised). When she left the party just minutes after midnight, she'd stood outside in the frosty air and tried to hail a cab. Finally she went back inside the building, called for a taxi and sat on a velour bench in the lobby. After forty minutes, the cab pulled up, she climbed in and headed home, thirteen blocks away.

With her phone set to silent last night, she'd missed two calls that had come in while she was partying like a rock star. She listened to the first message. Britt, her college friend who called once a year at the holidays. Too, too busy during the year for even a ten-minute chat, she extolled the triumphs of her husband, her precious daughter, and even her cuter-than-anything-on-this-planet dog. Blah blah blah.

The other missed call was from Maxwell. Shit. She listened to the message.

"Julie, it's Maxwell. Sorry I've been unavailable, and Happy New Year! Call me anytime."

But maybe not at five-thirty in the morning, she thought. Was it a one-hour or two-hour time difference in Aspen? She didn't even know if he was still there. Whatever, she'd call him back later. Or wait until Monday? Too much to think about now. She turned over and went back to sleep.

**

The office was closed until Monday, but Julie ventured in around noon. She was surprised to find

Anthony at his desk. A driven young man who stayed late and often came in on weekends, Anthony had a large cardboard cup of coffee on his desk. Dammit. She'd have to make a pot.

"Happy New Year, Miz Tate," he said. He wasn't solicitous, just mannered. Julie knew that about him and liked him for it. Anthony Mignacci was twenty-seven, single, and had worked for PCM for about a year and a half.

"Happy New Year to you, Anthony, and what are you doing here? I mean, what am I doing here, right? I'm just stopping in for an hour or so."

"And I just wanted to get a few of these client letters out today. I know it'll be busy in here on Monday." Julie paused. Anthony was great with clients and had excellent financial planning sense for someone so young. She hoped he'd keep his job. Would his marital status mean he was more of a target?

"Well, don't stay all day," she said, walking into her office and closing the door behind her.

By ten, she was hungry. A banana for breakfast wasn't enough, and she still wasn't up to drinking coffee. She needed something more in her stomach before she telephoned Maxwell. Vegan Heaven was a block up the street. Julie sighed. Make the damn call, she instructed herself.

She listened as the phone rang. He picked up on the third ring.

"Yes."

Julie had dialed from work, so the number on his cell phone was likely the company's general number. He couldn't know for sure it was she who was calling.

"Maxwell, it's Julie. I hope this isn't a bad time."

"Never a bad time, Julie. Happy New Year."

"To you as well. Maxwell, you know I wouldn't bother you on your vacation unless it was important."

"I know that. We're actually flying back this afternoon. My daughter has a dance recital tomorrow."

"Well. I'm calling because I know you don't like surprises, and that's not something I would do to you on your first day back. I'm tendering my resignation today, and I couldn't submit it without speaking with you first."

He was silent for a moment, enough that Julie knew he was shocked. Well, of course he was. Everyone who knew Julie would be surprised.

"Another firm got you, didn't they?"

"What? No. No, not at all. I'm leaving to pursue something completely different."

"What would that be, Julie?" His tone was decidedly more formal.

She steeled her nerves before speaking. This man had been her greatest supporter as she rose within the firm. He valued her, she knew, and he'd likely consider this an act of treason, in spite of the letter.

"My business partner and I are buying a bed and breakfast in the Berkshires."

She waited. Was he laughing silently on the other end?

"Really." He drew out the word. "Well, I didn't see that coming. How long have you planned this?" Julie didn't know if it was better that she couldn't see his face.

"Not that long, actually. It's a farm that's been in my family for generations, and my brother doesn't want to run it anymore…"

"You're going to run a farm, too?

"No, but I'm buying the place. Um, I can be here until the end of January. I'll have my letter on your desk when you come back." Her ears were humming like a high-tension wire.

"Sure," he said in a clipped voice. "We'll speak on Monday. Thank you, Julie." Without waiting for her to say anything, he disconnected the call.

Julie slumped in her chair. Her body felt like a wet, limp noodle, and she realized she'd been holding herself rigid throughout the conversation.

Now I really need something to eat, she thought. She grabbed her jacket and walked to Anthony's desk. He was hunched over a file and she startled him when she laid a hand on his shoulder.

"I'm going for a little walk and I'll pick up something to eat. Can I get you anything?"

"Are you going to the coffee place?" He looked so hopeful, and she imagined he loved the cinnamon buns, too.

"No," she almost shouted. "No, somewhere different. You want a bagel?"

He shook his head. Dark hair tumbled over his forehead. He was cute, but he looked like a teenager. "I'll get something from the vending machine. Thanks anyway." He turned back to his file.

"Back in a bit. Hold down the fort," she called over her shoulder.

***

She finished work and told Anthony she was heading home. Back in her apartment, she ran a bath and climbed into hot and bubbly goodness. She felt herself relax and wished she'd poured a glass of wine first.

After an hour's soak, she bundled into a thick robe and poured that glass of wine. It was late, and she thought about calling Tommy, but he hadn't phoned her, and he could have, dammit, so forget it. Her married friends were either out or already in bed. She'd already had her obligatory holiday conversations with Don, Eric, and even Ella out in San Diego.

Julie held her glass by its long stem and watched as candlelight danced inside the pale yellow wine. Was she about to make the biggest mistake of her life? She barely knew Zack and Sarah, had never conducted business with Freddy, other than when she'd hired him. She was about to leave Manhattan to live in Dalton, and although some changes had come to the small town where she'd grown up, western Massachusetts was still rural, especially compared to the city. Would her cultural tastes shrivel up? Where was the nearest Indian restaurant?

As the youngest of the five children, Julie was protected, mostly by Tommy but also in other ways by Don, Eric, and Ella. They viewed her as the baby, even at thirty-four, and while they all professed great admiration for her professional accomplishments, she surmised that they had no idea how hard she'd worked to achieve her status at PCM. To earn the big salary, and to save most of it so she'd have security. And now, she was about to risk that security so she could take over Jingle Valley. Would they even understand? None of them wanted to hang on to the past. But for Julie, it was something to be treasured and preserved.

THOMAS

Thomas rose early and quietly slipped from Maria's bed so as not to wake her. He gathered up his clothes and tip-toed into the adjoining bathroom, where he dressed. He hadn't brought his toothbrush, but found a bottle of mouthwash in a cupboard under the sink and took a swig from the bottle. He swished the liquid around in his mouth for as long as he could stand it before spitting in the sink.

He hadn't planned on spending the night, but their kissing on the couch had turned into something more, and it was she who had led him by the hand into her bedroom. As he zipped up his jeans he felt a piercing stab of guilt. They'd had a great time last night, and she was generous and giving. But…but…his chest felt tight, constricted. He needed air.

He raked his fingers through his hair and walked silently across thick carpet to her door. Carefully turning the deadbolt, he opened the door and stepped into the hallway, holding his shoes in his free hand. He knew she'd never forgive him for walking out, and yet he couldn't stop himself. What the hell was he running from?

He pulled the door shut behind him, slid his feet into topsiders and ran like hell to his car, full of regret.

JULIE

New Year. New beginnings. As Julie did every January first for the past ten years, she started a diet and cleaned out her closet.

No more carbs for the month. She made this promise aloud, even though no one was around to witness her proclamation and possibly call her out on it when she slipped. By February she'd be living in Dalton, and she knew she'd be eating carbs again. Sushi? Not likely. Tandoori chicken? Probably not. There'd be comfort food to get her through the winter, and that meant spaghetti, potatoes, bread. So no carbs for January.

She cleaned out her closet because she wouldn't need a lot of the pieces in Dalton. Boots and jeans and sweaters, yes. Not that she was ready to throw away (or donate) her fancy red-soled pumps and six black cocktail dresses (they were so different, she had rationalized with each purchase), but she couldn't take everything.

Freddy called around two.

"Good morning," he said in a flat voice.

"Hey you," Julie said. "Belated Happy New Year."

"Yeah," he said dully. "Happy freakin' new freakin' year."

"Uh-oh, that doesn't sound good. You looked so happy when I left the party last night. You were with that guy – what's his name?"

She heard Freddy exhale on the other end. "His name? His name is Curious George. As in, I might like to see what this lifestyle is like."

"Oh no. A dabbler? Want to come over? Are you hungry?"

"I'm starving. I haven't eaten since yesterday. Fat lot of good it did me to deny myself food in a vain effort to have a flat stomach."

"Okay, let's get out of our apartments. Where?"

"Can we go to MOMA? I don't want to see anyone I know."

Julie almost laughed out loud. Freddy ran into friends and acquaintances wherever he went. The Museum of Modern Art would be no exception. If he wanted to avoid people, he'd have to go…well, to Dalton, Massachusetts.

"Sure. Meet you in an hour."

"Half hour. Two-thirty."

"Okay, okay."

She pulled on her short boots and grabbed her bag. If she walked fast, she could get there in thirty minutes. There were still a lot of tourists in the city, finishing up the last weekend of the Christmas-to-New Year's holiday period.

He was there, waiting. Of course he was. She had jogged the last block and had to stop to catch her breath.

"What, did you run here? You should have arrived sooner if you ran."

"I didn't run, you idiot. I walked. Just let me catch my breath."

"You should take a boxing class with me," Freddy said. Julie glared up at him, all fit in jeans and work boots, dashing in a brown leather jacket. Freddy was so masculine looking, women were fooled all the time. Hell, Julie was fooled once, so deluded she'd come on to him. He'd actually played along, enjoying the attention, no doubt, until she'd leaned in for a soft kiss.

"I love women, and men," he'd whispered. Too caught up in the moment, she'd simply nodded and leaned in closer. With her glossy lips only centimeters from his, Freddy had cupped her chin and said, "But I love men more. And in a very special way." Then he'd brushed her cheeks with his lips while Julie processed this new, startling information. He loved to remind her of her deep affection for him whenever it suited his agenda.

She held her arms open and fell into his embrace. "So, tell me about Curious George," she said, her face against his jacket. He let her go and looked over her head at the few tourists on the street.

"No. I don't want to waste any more words on Boy George. Besides, he couldn't put a sentence together, and knew nothing about art or literature."

"Sports guy?"

"Oh yeah. With a man cave," Freddy scoffed. "Recently separated from his wife and, ugh…"

"Curious," Julie said, linking her arm through his. "Come on, let's enrich ourselves." She led him inside the museum.

***

Over New Year's Day salads, they discussed the upcoming move.

"So you gave notice over the telephone," Freddy said, wiping his mouth. "How did Max take it?"

Freddy had met Maxwell once, and called him Max then, and Maxwell corrected him with a sneery "It's actually Maxwell." Ever since then, Freddy insisted on calling him 'Max,' and Julie made sure the two of them never crossed paths again.

"He took it, and since it was a phone conversation, I couldn't read his face, but I imagine he was taken by surprise," Julie said, nodding as the waiter held a pot of coffee over her empty cup. "At first he thought another firm had lured me away, although I don't think anywhere else would pay me as much. When I told him I was moving to the family farm to run a B&B, he said we'd speak next week and ended the conversation. I could practically see him rolling his eyes on the other end."

"And I'm sure he got on the phone immediately with a headhunter to find your replacement."

"Whatever. The die is cast," she said with a dramatic wave of her hand. "It makes leaving easier. What about you?"

Freddy had worked for a construction firm years ago, but had endured numerous layoffs and eventually struck out on his own. Usually he had enough high-end work to keep him well-fed, usually from Upper East Side housewives eager for a new kitchen, and when Freddy gave one a written estimate of $75,000, she just said,

"Give it to my husband." But lately the calls were fewer. And Freddy had grown tired of the excess, the extravagant spending. *Two* Sub-zero refrigerators, *two* Bosch dishwashers, a six-burner Russell range. For people who don't even cook.

"I can't wait to start renovating that barn," he said with an impish grin.

"Yeah, well, I'm not letting you go wild with a hammer and chain saw, Freddy Kruger."

THOMAS

Thomas hid in the guest house all day. He told Linda he was sick, a stomach bug of some sort, and she stayed away, only leaving a pot of tea and a tureen of chicken broth at his doorstep. Thomas knew she'd find out soon enough; Maria would call her. But his own phone stayed silent all day, which Thomas knew was an ominous sign. She must really be mad.

And why wouldn't she be? He was an idiot and a cad. They'd had a wonderful night, and he liked her a lot. She was warm, witty, sexy, and playful – everything he could wish for, and now he'd blown any chance of being with her again by bolting from her bed at sunrise.

There was a knock on his door. Thomas had pulled the shades, and no one could peek in through the window at the side or the small window in his front door. He walked to the door.

"Who is it?"

"It's your brother. Open up."

"Donnie, I feel like shit."

"I don't care. Open the damn door now."

Thomas obeyed and opened the door, squinting against the bright Arizona winter sun. Don pushed past him and entered the guest house, glaring at the unmade bed, the scattered clothing on the floor.

"Look at this place," he spat.

"I could use a maid," said Thomas, realizing too late that Don was in no mood for jokes.

"You're a jerk, you know that?" He pushed some clothes off the one chair in the room and sat, crossing his ankle over his knee.

Thomas slumped on the bed. "Yeah, I know."

"She called Linda in tears. Couldn't understand why you'd spend the night and then creep out in the morning without a word. Jeez, Tommy."

Thomas cupped his head in his hands. "I know." He looked up at his older brother. "Donnie, I don't know why I ran. I really like her."

"What the hell are you scared of? Being happy?" Don's dark eyes blazed with fury.

"Maybe. Maybe that's exactly what I'm scared of. That I don't deserve someone like her."

"Well, you don't. Not now, at least. Look, Linda and I, we've had our share. Everybody does. I've pissed her off plenty, but either you stay and make things right or you cut bait." Don rose to his feet, standing tall over his brother. He squeezed Thomas's shoulder, hard, until Thomas winced and looked up.

"Fix this situation. Now. My wife is livid at all male Tates right now. Tomorrow you need to find your own place. Time to grow up," he said as he slammed the door behind him.

JULIE

Julie arrived at work early on Monday morning, hoping to get there before Maxwell. But no chance of it. He probably slept here last night, she thought.

She'd avoided CoffeeX on her way in, not even glancing over as she hurried by. Axel was probably in the kitchen anyway, making those stupid cinnamon buns. Didn't matter, she told herself as she entered her office building, she wasn't eating carbs all month.

Maxwell's secretary Kendra must have been keeping an eye out for her, because Julie had no sooner shrugged off her coat than her phone's intercom buzzed.

"Yes?" she said after pressing the button.

"Julie, Maxwell is waiting for you in his office."

"Be right there." Not a moment to waste, right? And she hadn't even had one sip of coffee yet.

She scribbled a note and stuck it on Harmony's computer. *In with M. Get me a giant coffee pls! x*

Maxwell's office was in the front corner of the building, opposite Julie's, which was in the windowless back. Julie walked with purpose, past empty cubicles that in an hour would be filled with young men and women on the phone, on the computer. Little hamsters on a corporate treadmill. She glanced at Kendra, who used her head to point at Maxwell's closed door. "Go ahead," she indicated before returning to furious key-pounding.

Julie rapped twice and opened the door to Maxwell's luxurious office. He had all the trappings of a CEO:

plush carpeting, replaced every eighteen months, subtle but expensive art on the walls, the best furniture. He was standing in front of the window when she walked in. Tall and slender, Maxwell's hair covered his shirt collar, and was mostly silver now. He turned and Julie stared. He'd shaved off his mustache and goatee and looked ten years younger.

"Wow! I like the look," she said, hoping for a cheery welcome. His tone on the telephone last week had made her nervous about this meeting. But he smiled and swept out his arm in a gesture telling her to sit. She lowered herself into one of two oversized leather chairs and was surprised when, instead of taking his customary seat behind his desk, he sat in the matching chair and faced her.

"Thanks. New Year's Day decision. That and no carbs, of course."

"Of course," she murmured.

"So, Julie. Big plans ahead for you. You're going to be an innkeeper." The corners of his mouth turned up slightly, and she felt her face get warm. She wished she could control the involuntary blush.

She licked her lips. Her mouth had gone dry in the past two minutes. "That's right. A new chapter for me." She would not look down, and held his gaze until he averted his eyes. Ha, she thought. I win. "After receiving Barton's email, this decision was easier for me. And I'm looking forward to the new challenges."

"Yes, adventure and challenge. Now, in our earlier conversation, you indicated staying until the end of the month, correct?"

"Right. I want to be here to assist with the transition."

"That probably won't be necessary. I'm bringing Candace Russell up from Miami. She should be here Thursday night, and ready to go." Maxwell inspected his fingernails.

Candace Russell had worked for Julie until a year and a half ago, when she relocated to run the much-smaller Miami office. They'd never gotten along, and Julie was surprised Maxwell would select her. Candace had a penchant for pursuing married men, and Julie remembered Candace's transfer to Miami came at the same time her affair with Winfield C. Slocum IV was exposed. Win Slocum, scion of the venerable Slocum real estate dynasty, hadn't been seen at social events since. His wife Willow was said to be living year-round at the Newport "cottage."

"Oh, that's great. Candace is a good choice." What else could she say? At least she wouldn't need training.

"Yes," Maxwell said softly. "I'm sorry to see you go, Julie. You've been an asset to the company. But Friday will be your last day. Kendra will get all the necessary paperwork to you by tomorrow."

Friday? "This Friday, Maxwell? I can stay on. I'd planned to stay on, until the end of the month." But even as she said it, she knew the deal. He wanted her gone. If

Candace had arrived this past weekend, today would have been her last day.

"We'll be fine, Julie," he said, tapping her knee as if she were seven. He stood, a signal that their meeting was over.

Julie extended her hand to her boss, grasped it firmly, and let go.

THOMAS

The dozen roses hadn't worked, apparently. Thomas couldn't blame Maria for wanting nothing to do with him, but he had to try.

She was back at school now; classes had started up again after the holiday break. And Thomas knew Don was dead serious when he'd demanded that Thomas find an apartment.

Thomas sent a text to Julie, asking her to sell his truck. He needed a car now. Buttoning his shirt and tucking it into pressed khaki trousers, he made his way across the patio and entered the kitchen through the back door. Linda mumbled a good morning to him and filled his mug with coffee.

"Linda, I'm a fool. I know that. But I'm going to try and fix this."

"Some things can't be fixed. You hurt that girl, Tom. You treated her like she was expendable."

"I know I did. And I don't blame her for not wanting anything to do with me right now." He blew on the steaming coffee before taking a sip. "But I'm determined to make it right with Maria." He exhaled and squared his shoulders. "I need to find an apartment, but first I need a car. I'm going to lease something."

"Sounds good," Linda said, not lifting her head as she worked a crossword puzzle.

"Any chance you could give me a lift to one of the dealers? I don't really care at this point. Toyota, Honda, even Hyundai would be fine."

She glanced up. "I can drop you at the Honda place when I head out." She raised her eyes to the clock on the wall. "Half hour from now."

"Sure, that'll be fine. Thanks." He picked up his mug of coffee and stood. "I'll take this back with me and get my stuff."

"Nothing to eat?"

He paused. The kitchen was clean. Linda had made no move to cook for him, as she'd done every morning up until New Year's.

"Nah, I'm good. See you in a half hour."

JULIE

Julie returned to her office to find Harmony setting a tall cardboard cup on her desk. And a cookie.

"Thanks, Harm," she said. "But no cookie for me. Keep it. I'm dieting."

"You? Come on, you don't need to. Now me, I'll eat the cookie and gain five pounds." She picked up the cookie, still wrapped in waxed paper, and turned to leave.

"Harm, wait. Sit down a minute."

Harmony turned back, a puzzled expression on her round face. "What happened in Maxwell's office just now? Everything okay?"

Julie leaned forward, resting her elbows on her desk. Harmony had worked for her now for almost five years, and she'd developed into a top-notch assistant. This would be hard.

"Harm, I gave my notice to Maxwell. I thought I'd be staying until the end of the month, but actually, my last day will be Friday."

Harmony leaned hard against the door frame, then took two steps forward and fell into the chair opposite Julie's desk. Then she jumped to her feet, dropping the cookie on Julie's desk. It broke into pieces.

"This is a joke, right? New Year's joke?" She shook her head so violently that her dark hair swung back and forth, slapping at her cheeks. She began to pace.

Julie moved from behind her desk to stand in front of her, using her foot to push the door shut. She reached out and rubbed Harmony's shoulders, a soothing gesture she remembered her dad used to do. Harmony grabbed her in a hug and let out a choking sob.

"Please, Julie, please don't go. I don't know what I'll do without you. I hate everyone else here," she whimpered into Julie's shoulder.

Julie smiled, still in Harmony's desperate embrace. She didn't much care for anyone in the office, either. She and Harmony were a team.

Julie extricated herself from the hug and placed her hands again on Harmony's soft upper arms. "You're going to be fine," she said in the most convincing voice she could muster.

"Take me with you!" Harmony's watery eyes brightened. "Where are you going? McKenzie Jackson? Sherman and Patrick?"

Julie tilted her head to the side, the way a mom would do when she was trying to find the best way to tell her daughter that the goldfish died.

"I'm going to Dalton, Massachusetts, to my family's farm. I'm going to run it as an event venue, you know, weddings and parties." Julie waited for the words to settle in Harmony's brain.

"Get out! Seriously? Julie, that is awesome!" In spite of her desolation, and wet cheeks, Harmony couldn't contain her excitement at the news. "I love that idea!"

"Me, too, honey. And I can't wait for you to come up and visit. Your first stay is on me."

"Wow. You are the coolest person I know." Harmony swept a strand of hair away from her damp cheek.

Ha, thought Julie, still smiling.

***

The week went by, too quickly, and suddenly it was Friday. Julie had spent an hour on Thursday afternoon packing up her office and finalizing paperwork. She was surprised to find that everything she'd had in her office, everything that was personal, not corporate, could fit into one cardboard box. With the cover on.

On Friday morning she arrived at work, by-passing CoffeeX again (forget Axel, she thought, that was so over). Candace Russell, her replacement, might already be there, setting her coffee mug on the desk and ordering new business cards. Julie had had no contact with Candace in the past eighteen months, had no idea what was going on in Candace's life.

Her office was empty, but there were two new framed photos on the back table. Julie never kept personal photographs in her office. Sure, some people thought it was important – the CEO who wanted to appear familial, paternal. The guy who worked twelve hours a day pitching annuities had a photo of his wife and newborn son on his desk, probably to remind him why he was working so hard. Even when Christopher was in her life, she didn't bring in a photograph of him to display on her desk for everyone to see and gossip about.

She peered at the photographs. One of Candace accepting some kind of award, shaking the hand of a tall, thin man in a dark suit. Her hair was longer and blonder than Julie recalled. The other picture was of Candace standing behind a podium. Yep, all about Candy. Julie pulled her phone from her big bag and texted Harmony. *Could u pick up a coffee for me pls?* There was an immediate reply. *Sure*

Julie sat in her chair and laid her palms on the bare desk. She opened each of her drawers again, checking one last time that she'd removed all her personal items. She knew this day would be difficult, perhaps not so much for the emotions involved in leaving a job after nine years. The hardest part would be in dealing with Candace, in smiling through the day, and in saying one last goodbye to Harmony. Julie supposed it was better than being escorted out of the building, with a security guard at your elbow, a cardboard box of your possessions already packed. Or going through layoffs the way Freddy had, layoffs that some of her co-workers would experience soon. Julie expected one final paycheck, direct deposited to her checking account, and a separate deposit for her unused vacation time. Her health insurance would be covered through the end of the month.

She'd been contacted by Tommy's lawyer, a Mr. Robert Gleason. The name sounded vaguely familiar, and Julie surmised he was the same lawyer who'd handled her parents' legal matters. After all, how many lawyers were there in Dalton, anyway? The paperwork to buy Tommy out of the farm looked fine, and after consulting with Brenda, her attorney friend, she'd signed everything necessary, then FedEx'd it all back. So that was that. Her bank had no problem with the financing. Once she was settled and Freddy had joined her, she'd contact Mr.

Gleason again and have him add Freddy's name to the deed, but she didn't want Tommy to know that until after the fact. She simply didn't want to have to defend their decision to Tommy.

"Knock knock!" The loud, smoky voice of Candace Russell startled her. And there she was, looming in the doorway of Julie's office. Julie stood, stepped away from her desk, even though technically it was still her desk. Can-do Candy, that was the name Julie had given her when they first met. She imagined Candace had other, more unsavory nicknames. The Miami sun had aged Candace's face, Julie could see. She'd be sorry: the sun and those cigarettes she still smoked, from the smell emanating off her clothes, would catch up with her soon.

"Hey," Julie said, hoping to avoid an embrace. They each made a kissing noise into the air next to the other's cheek and pulled apart quickly.

"So I bet you thought you'd never see me again," Candace said, tossing two bags on the floor next to Julie's desk. One was a Michael Kors purse, a python satchel that Julie knew retailed for about three thousand. The other was a forty-dollar canvas tote from LL Bean that was filthy. Julie almost laughed out loud.

Candace began unloading the tote: black pumps, to replace the leopard-print vinyl boots she was wearing, a one-liter bottle of water, a woolen (or likely cashmere) scarf, a green ceramic coffee cup with the firm's logo on it, and, yep, three framed photographs that Candace set on the desk, facing down.

"How was your flight?" Julie edged toward the door, praying Harmony would arrive soon so she'd have an excuse to, well, excuse herself.

"Long. Stupid weather up here. And there was a bratty kid on the plane. God, if they weren't paying me a fortune to move here, I'd never have come back. I miss Miami!" she whined. It was like a caricature, Julie thought.

"I remember you never liked the snow," Julie said, glancing out the window at the gray sky. Manhattan usually got rain instead of snow, but all the forecasts were predicting that this winter would be especially harsh. Julie didn't care – she'd been raised on New England winters, but Candace? What a shame, she thought happily.

"Is there coffee? Do I have a secretary?" She stretched her neck to peek out the doorway. Julie walked out of the office and noticed that Harmony had moved her desk. Julie could always see Harmony when she was seated; they could actually talk to each other without getting up, and they did, often. Now Harmony's desk was about a foot to the left, and Candace wouldn't be able to see her. Julie stifled a smile.

"You have an excellent *assistant*, Harmony. She'll be in soon. Her day starts at eight-thirty."

Candace snorted. "Her day's about to start a lot earlier."

Julie stared at her. Poor Harm. She was going to hate this new regime, and probably hate Julie for leaving.

THOMAS

Thomas had a car and now he had his own apartment. He signed a lease for a Civic and as soon as the ink was dry, he drove it off the lot and straight to Maria's apartment complex in what he learned was the North Gateway area of Phoenix. The building manager showed him a model apartment, one bedroom, same as Maria's, and he said he'd take it. Just like that. He liked hers, and was too unfamiliar with any of the other complexes in the area.

"Of course, we'll need to run a credit check, all that annoying stuff," the manager said. She smiled big and bobbed her head as she filled out forms for Thomas to sign. She had introduced herself as Betty Anne Hollis, assistant property manager.

"Sure, that's no problem. I just moved here last month, but I start work at the Desert Resort Golf Course at the end of the month. And I can cover first, last, security, whatever you need, Ms. Hollis."

"Betty Anne, please! Canyon Crossroads is a lovely place. Lots of singles here," she added with a wink.

"Yeah," Thomas murmured, thinking of Maria. How would she react when she learned he'd rented an apartment six doors down the hall?

"Now, are you going to move in at the end of the month?"

"I'd like to move in as soon as possible," he said. His next stop would be the furniture store. There was a furnished unit available, but Thomas had made up his mind. He was staying here in Phoenix. He'd have his own bed.

JULIE

"Freddy, I want to go to the farm. I'll go out of my mind if I don't do something. I've packed up most of my stuff and now I'm just pacing."

"I'll come with you," he said. "Are we taking the train?"

"I thought I'd rent one of those U-Haul trucks."

"Oh! So, like a real move then. Can you drive it?" Freddy laughed on the other end, and Julie made a face he couldn't see.

"Not if it's a standard. But you can," she said and held her breath.

"You need me. You so need me," he taunted.

"You're right. Can you be away for a few days?"

"I'm planning to be away forever!" he cried. "Well, maybe not forever, but for a long time. I'm in this with you, Jules. I may end up being celibate for years, but I'm in this."

"What, you don't think there are any available guys in the Berkshires? Are you kidding, Freddy?"

"Well…maybe in Stockbridge, not in Dalton."

"We'll both be too busy to have sex, anyway," she said.

"Stop it."

***

Julie secured rental of the truck, and together she and Freddy loaded cardboard boxes secured with duct tape, a rocking chair, microwave oven (Tommy loathed them), and four portable closets. Then they drove the truck to Freddy's apartment, where they loaded even more. Julie had contacted a housing services organization, whose volunteers arrived at dawn to haul away the heavier furniture.

With Freddy behind the wheel and Julie next to him, they took off, leaving Manhattan behind them for the foreseeable future.

"Want to sing 'Old MacDonald' with me?" Freddy shifted gears and headed north.

Two hours later, they stopped for a bathroom break.

"I'm starving," Julie said. "Look, let's just grab something here before we get back on the road. There's at least another hour to go, probably more with the traffic back in Yonkers."

Freddy looked around at the rest stop. "Where the hell are we?"

"Winsted."

"Connecticut or Massachusetts?" He arched his back, turning his face to the cloudless sky, letting the weak winter sun touch his cheeks.

"Connecticut. But we're almost to Massachusetts." She turned as a couple walked past them. "Excuse me, do you know of any place nearby where we could get some lunch?"

The elderly couple directed them to Main Street, a place called Huckleberry's.

"Great," Freddy muttered. "I can only imagine. Old people food. Creamed corn and meatloaf."

"Stop it. We need to eat. You know, you could have a better attitude."

"Oh, please don't let this be our first fight," Freddy said, grabbing Julie in a bear hug. "I was hoping our first big blow-out would be on the farm."

She wrestled away from him and grinned. "Shut up and drive."

***

By the time they finally turned onto the long road that led to Jingle Valley, it was nearly two. The anemic sun was already behind the tallest pines. Daylight didn't last long in the valley, especially not in winter. Julie knew Freddy was tired. He could drive the U-Haul, but he wasn't used to it. They'd both need to acclimate themselves to driving everywhere. She'd miss all the walking she did in Manhattan, but figured she'd get plenty of exercise in this new life.

"Here we are," she stated as Freddy shifted into park.

"Here we are." He sat but didn't move. Julie kept quiet. She should have brought him up here for a walk-around inspection first. She was sure he was having second thoughts. Well, Freddy's a big boy and he made his own decision, she reminded herself. She reached over and took his hand.

"We'll be fine. We'll be great."

"Gonna have the whole world on a plate," Freddy sang. He turned his face to her and Julie touched his stubbly cheek. She loved him so much. They *would* be swell, she could feel it. The start of something big.

They stepped out of the truck and Julie crunched over an inch of icy snow on her way to retrieve the house key.

Freddy pointed. "Is that Tom's truck? We could use it." He looked around the open stalls that served as a garage. "There should be doors here," he said. "I'll add it to the list."

"He asked me to sell it. We can just buy it. I imagine he's already got himself a car out in Phoenix," Julie said as she picked up the big rock and plucked the house key from its earthen bed. She opened the door to the kitchen and held it ajar for Freddy. "Let's get our bearings before we start unloading the U-Haul."

"Sure. We can return it tomorrow. Then we can start using Tommy's."

"Yeah," Julie said, sniffing the air, convinced she could smell apple pie again. Had Sarah been here?

Freddy stood in the kitchen, his head nearly bumping the ceiling, and surveyed. "This space should be okay for making breakfasts. No dinner, though." With his finger, he pointed up. "Bed," and pointed to the stove. "And breakfast. I can't wait to see the barn."

"Box lunches for day trips?"

"Sure." He walked into the main dining room and flattened his palms on the big table. "This needs to go," he stated. Seeing Julie's face, he explained. "Better to have smaller tables set up around the room. A couple in love doesn't want to sit at a big table with other folks."

"You're right," she said. "But this table's been in my family for a long time."

Freddy stood in front of her and lifted her chin with his finger. "Look at me," he instructed. "We have to make a lot of changes to turn this old farmhouse into a B&B. We'll talk everything out, but you have to be flexible about this, okay?"

Julie nodded wordlessly.

"Maybe I can find a use for the table in the barn," he soothed. "I'm going to do a quick walk-through." He left her alone in the dining room.

Julie touched the polished wood of the table. Where would this go? Into storage? Should she sell it? She couldn't sell it. Maybe Freddy could put it in the barn somewhere. The table seated twelve without the extra leaves; there was plenty of space in this room to fit four to six tables. Why wouldn't people want to sit together at this table? That's what B&Bs are all about, she told herself. No, the table would stay. She rapped it with her knuckles for good luck.

"Jules, come here quick!" At the urgency in Freddy's voice, Julie hurried down the hall to the master bedroom.

"What is it?" she asked, following his gaze to the ceiling.

Freddy's index finger showed the way to the upper corner of the plastered ceiling. "See that? Water damage." He spun around and faced her.

"Well, I didn't do it! And where? I don't see anything up there." She squinted again at the supposed damage.

Freddy grabbed her hand and led her to stand in the corner. "Look up," he commanded. "Someone tried to camouflage it. Probably sprayed bleach to whiten out the stain." He clucked his tongue. "Thomas," he muttered.

"Okay," Julie stated. "Okay, so what does that mean? We can fix it, right?" She pulled her hand away from Freddy's.

"I'll need to see how bad it is first," he said. "Come on, follow me upstairs."

He strode out of the bedroom and headed toward the back staircase, then took the steps two at a time with his long legs. Julie hurried after him.

In one of the two upstairs bathrooms (the larger one, the one with the claw foot tub), Freddy lowered himself to the floor and stuck a hand under the tub. Julie chewed a fingernail and said nothing, but her mind raced. She saw dollar signs in every crack – in the old tub, the floor, the windowpane. She had funds set aside for renovations, but how much would she need?

He slid out and washed his hands at the white pedestal sink before turning back to her.

"There's rot, definitely. Might have to take out the tub and put a new floor in," he said, hands in the back pockets of his jeans. "And then the pipes. You gotta figure, Jules, people won't stay in a place where they have to worry about the shower, the tub, or the toilet."

Julie glanced out the small bathroom window. A cobweb clung to the upper corner of the frame. Smoke spiraled up from the chimney of the little house at the edge of the farm, where Zack and Sarah lived. She watched the trail rise until it became one with the ashen sky.

"Jules?"

"Yeah, I heard you." She turned back to face Freddy. "Did we make a horrible mistake?"

Freddy smiled, that crooked lazy smile that sent her stomach doing flip-flops the first time they met. He stuck out his long arms and rested big, heavy hands on her shoulders. Pulling her close, he wrapped her up against him. "Ssh," he whispered. "We'll be fine. I can do whatever repairs need to be done, and I've got a couple of guys who can come up for the big projects." He pulled away and grinned. "Let's have tea."

***

Freddy was right about the repairs. There were repairs to be done in just about every room. Together they made a list and estimated the cost of materials. It was discouraging – their resources would take a huge hit.

"So why did Tommy bail, anyway? Did he ever tell you the truth?" Freddy asked over tea.

Julie lifted a shoulder and let it sag back down. "I think he just gave up trying," she said, blowing on her tea before taking a tentative sip. "His heart was never into it, you know. He always thought Eric should have been running this place, and if not Eric, then me. The girl," she added with an eye roll. "Tommy took it on because he felt obligated to, not because he wanted to. He wasn't much of a handyman, and I'm guessing he used whatever income he had to do things besides repairs. You know, like pay for electricity and food."

"Remember how I said there'd be more money in weddings than in just a B&B?"

Julie nodded.

"Well, I've been thinking," Freddy said. "We can go ahead and fix this place up, sure. We'd be using a lot of money on the house. But I don't know if we'll see a return on the investment." He leaned forward and laid a warm hand on Julie's forearm. "We've got six bedrooms in the house, but only four to rent out, since we need our own space. It would be…*unusual* to have all four bedrooms filled at once, and even if we did, I don't know that we'd make enough to cover expenses." He leaned back in his chair.

"So what are you saying? How can we have weddings here without a place for people to stay?"

"There are plenty of decent inns in Pittsfield and Lenox. I say we make the minimal repairs on the house so that you and I can live and work here. We focus on the barn. It's big enough for a good-sized wedding. I get my guys up here and we construct a commercial kitchen in the back, and add the honeymoon suite I'd talked about on the upper level. That's where we make our money." His dark eyes looked as though they were backlit and his fingers danced on the table. "And, we have to get rid of the animals."

"Get rid of the animals!" Julie's hand flew to her open mouth, but Freddy kept talking.

"Sell them, sweetie, sell them." He waited for Julie to lower her hand. "Look, I'd rather we utilize our renovation budget in the smartest way possible." Julie watched him closely as he spoke.

"I remember attending a wedding up in Waitsfield, probably seven or eight years ago. The Round Barn, I think it was?" Julie asked. "And there were buses to transport guests back to the hotel." She nodded as she remembered the event.

"Yes! I know about that place. We can use it as a model for what we want to do here. This barn can hold up to two hundred, I bet, and we could turn it into a beautiful place." Freddy stopped to take a breath. "We keep the house for us. Instead of sinking all of our money into the house, we'll build the kitchen and the honeymoon suite. I'll get the professional help we need to do this right."

His enthusiasm was infectious. Julie began to feel something, a tingle, an increase in her pulse. A promise. "Weddings at Jingle Valley Farm," she said slowly. "Dalton's premier destination!"

"Right? Look around, all this land. We sell off the animals. I can work inside the house this month while it's cold, fix what needs fixing. Then I'll bring up a couple of my buddies to work on the barn once we have the plans in place. Julie, just imagine!"

Julie's feet bounced silently on the kitchen floor, under the big wooden table. "Freddy, you're a genius."

"I want this place to work, for both of us. We're partners. And we're good." He grinned.

Julie pushed her chair back and stood up. She held out her arms and waited for Freddy to stand as well.

They embraced and both began jumping up and down, softly at first, then harder, faster.

"Weddings at Jingle Valley!" Julie raised her arms in the air.

"A Jingle Valley wedding. Memorable," Freddy crooned.

THOMAS

Thomas couldn't bake to save his life, but he found a European patisserie a couple of miles from his new apartment and bought an assortment of small, delectable pastries. At eleven o'clock on a sunny Saturday morning, he stood outside Maria's apartment and knocked gently. This could be the stupidest thing I've ever done, he thought. What if she's not alone? What if she's not home? I can't leave this box on the floor. He heard the lock turn and she opened the door. God, she looked pretty, he thought.

"Thomas," she said flatly.

"Hi. I hope this isn't a bad time," Thomas said, trying to see past her into the apartment.

"What do you want?" Her voice was small, and she sounded more sad than angry.

"To apologize," he said. He held out the box. "I thought maybe we could talk. Please, Maria."

She glanced at the box, then back at him. After a long few seconds, she stepped back and opened the door. "Come in," she said before turning away from him. He stepped over the threshold and followed her, closing the door behind him.

"I'll make a pot of coffee. You can set that down here," she said, gesturing to the granite countertop that looked the same as the one in his new apartment. Thomas thought it better not to mention that he was now her neighbor. Not yet. Let's see how the making-up part goes first, he thought.

"Thanks." He watched her go through the motions of filling the pot with cold water, placing a paper filter in the basket, measuring out coffee from a bag she pulled off a shelf. She pushed a button to start the coffeemaker and turned to him.

"That's a good place, Claudine's." She took a pair of scissors from a drawer and snipped the string that held the box together. Thomas held his breath. He knew she liked dark chocolate, and hoped she'd be pleased with his selection.

Maria lifted her eyes to him. "Tell me why you came here, Thomas."

He perched on a stool, one of two that were at the counter. "I bolted. Ran like a scared little boy. And I've hated myself ever since." He turned his hands over so the palms were facing up. "Maria, I'm sorry. Really. It was a foolish, childish thing for me to do." He was surprised when his throat tightened and he swallowed hard.

"You disrespected me. How else can I put it? I thought we liked each other. And I didn't ask for any more from you, did I?"

Thomas shook his head. He had no words. The pressure behind his eyes made him blink. Now she'd think he was faking tears, dammit.

The coffee was ready. He sat silently as she filled two ceramic mugs. His mug was bright yellow with a dark blue star and the words "Best Teacher" printed on it. Hers was white with "Santa Fe" emblazoned in bold red letters.

"How do you take your coffee?"

"This is fine, thanks," he said. But he didn't drink. "I want to make it up to you. However long it takes. To prove to you that I do care, that I would do anything if you'd give me another chance."

"First tell me why you left. All you've said is that it was stupid. Why did you feel it was necessary to sneak out of here?" She held him with her gaze.

He traced a fingertip along the rim of his mug. If he wasn't honest with her now, there would be nothing. No chance for the two of them. He looked up.

"I was married before."

"You've told me."

"It didn't work out. Mostly my fault, and I've had a lot of regrets that I was a poor excuse for a husband. We didn't communicate, I could have done a lot more to help that situation. It's been three years, Maria, and you were the first..." He used the heel of his hand to swipe at his eyes.

"I'm giving you another chance right now, Thomas. You're here, in my apartment."

Thomas exhaled. "Thank you. Would you let me take you to dinner?"

Maria sipped her coffee slowly before setting her mug back on the counter. Finally she replied.

"Maybe. Next weekend maybe. And I'm not playing games with you, you know."

Thomas nodded. He really should tell her about his apartment, but the situation seemed so fragile, as if they were encased in a big soap bubble and any movement could shatter it. But what if they ran into each other this coming week? It could happen.

"I need to tell you something else," Thomas said, straightening his shoulders.

She took a step back from the counter and folded her arms across her chest. Uh-oh, Thomas thought, there's a defensive stance if I ever saw one.

"What." Her dark eyes were flinty and her lips pressed into a thin horizontal line. God, she was beautiful, Thomas thought.

"Well, you know Linda was pretty pissed off with me, too, after…you know. She wanted me out of the house, which I totally understood. And I needed an apartment fast. And I like this one so much…"

"You moved in here?" She didn't uncross her arms, and she didn't take her eyes off him.

"Yeah. I'm down the hall. I didn't plan it, honest. I had every intention of driving around and looking at other complexes. The rental agent here told me this was one of the only units available."

"So you're already living here," she said. "Next door?" Her perfectly arched eyebrows lifted almost to her hairline.

"Six doors down," he said, so low he almost didn't hear himself. Thomas took a gulp of coffee and stared at his shoes. Man, she likes strong coffee, he said to himself.

To his surprise, Maria laughed. Thomas looked up and she laughed again. Was she laughing at him?

"Well, I guess we'd better get along then," she said, as she filled his cup.

JULIE

Through the frigid month of January, Freddy worked inside the house. When he was upstairs, Julie stayed downstairs, polishing furniture, cleaning the oven and refrigerator. She'd drive to Pittsfield for groceries and whatever Freddy put on his list. She learned the difference between latex and oil-based paints, and even a paint for the bathroom that kept mildew away. In the evenings, Freddy worked on ideas for the barn transformation and Julie set up her office.

The farm animals were sold, to a guy Ethan knew. Ethan brokered the deal, and Julie was happy with the sale. It gave them a cash infusion and cleared the barn for Freddy to begin work in late February. He'd brought up an architect friend from New York to plan the renovations.

"This is an exceptional property," the architect, Gilles Orsino, had remarked after the initial tour. He wore a long sweeping coat that billowed behind him like an incoming wave. Freddy said Gilles had designed Chanticleer and GrottoBella, bistros that Julie checked online. They were stunning in their simplicity. And Freddy was able to convince Gilles to discount his rate. Julie didn't ask how, but Freddy said he'd need a weekend away soon. They looked good together, Julie thought, happy that at least one of them had a romance brewing.

The barn would be transformed into a two-level venue, and would hold up to two hundred twenty guests, even with a dance floor. On one side there would be space for a small band. A tiny chapel would be constructed where the horse stalls once stood, and a professional kitchen would be added in back. Gilles proposed keeping as much of the original wood as possible, adding wrought-iron chandeliers and hidden heating and air-conditioning ducts so as to be unobtrusive to guests. He and Freddy spent days together, and Freddy often left the house in the evening to drive Gilles back to his hotel in Pittsfield. He'd return early the next morning, when Julie was still in bed but awake.

One morning over coffee, after Gilles had returned to Manhattan, Julie asked, "So, Gilles?" She used her best French accent to pronounce his name.

Freddy lowered his lashes and Julie smiled as his cheeks flushed. "Yeah, Gilles."

"Come on, that's great!" she said, meaning it.

Freddy shrugged. "It won't last, I can tell. He and I hit it off, but it'll end soon. I'm here, he's back there. You know how that usually goes."

"Aren't you going away with him in a couple of weeks?"

"Yeah, he's got a time share in Conway and asked me to come up."

"So that's good, right? You're doing better than I am, Fred."

"It's fine. But it's just for now. And right now it's fine. I'm not expecting more than that." He looked out the window.

"Okay. Well, I'd take a fine-for-right-now right about now."

Freddy grinned. "We'll find you someone. Want to get away from here tonight? There's a blues café in Lenox we could check out. Grab a bite first at that Thai place – remember we drove by it and you said we should go sometime?"

Julie smiled at her friend. Thank God for Freddy, she thought. "Perfect," she said.

"Great! I'm gonna go talk with Zack. You got anything for him or Sarah?"

Zack and Sarah had expressed concern that with the farm mostly gone, they'd be forced to move from the little house at the edge of the property. Julie had assured them that they were welcome to stay there as long as they wanted. Zack still worked for them, she reminded him, and he'd be a huge help as the barn went through its transformation. Although he wasn't skilled in construction, the grounds needed a lot of work, even with the land frozen. Sarah still did some baking, and Julie wanted to tap her talents as the kitchen crew was assembled. She didn't have formal training, but Julie wanted her to be included. Sarah expressed an interest in learning to make wedding cakes, and Julie offered to pay for a six-week class in Pittsfield. They were valued employees as well as friends.

"I picked up some of those figs Zack likes." She opened a cupboard and took a box from the shelf and handed it to him. "He'll be surprised."

"See you later," Freddy said as he headed out.

***

Freddy had his long weekend in the White Mountains with Gilles while Julie shopped for antiques and decorations for the honeymoon suite. Every night, she was exhausted from the physical work involved in turning a tired old farm that had been neglected for years into a vibrant wedding venue. She'd drop into bed, pull two blankets and a comforter up to her chin and wish there was body heat next to her to take away the chill. Any body heat at this point. Maybe she should get a dog. A big furry dog.

She tried not to think too much about her old job or her life back in Manhattan. There wasn't time, really. But every once in a while, lying in bed, staring at the blackness and not hearing the muffled sound of traffic, she'd reminisce about the way life was. She may not have had many dates, but Julie had always prepped for possibility. She rarely left her apartment without makeup, dressed carefully during the week, because she never knew if there would be an impromptu business meeting called, or someone to meet after work for a drink. There was always that chance, she recalled.

Yeah, maybe it wasn't so bad being out of the city. She dressed comfortably every day, wore minimal makeup, got plenty of exercise without having to trek to the gym. Julie nestled in deeper against the chill. She was trying to keep the heating bills down until they had some income, which was at least months away.

Zack had brought a friend over last week. A few years older meant he was still younger than Julie, but she didn't care. Freddy and Julie had invited Zack and Sarah over for dinner, a way of thanking them for all their work and loyalty. Zack had inquired if his friend Marc could join them. He was visiting from Montreal and Julie welcomed him into their home. She'd made vegetable lasagna after learning that Marc was a vegetarian, and added meatballs on the side for the carnivores. Marc was cute, clean-shaven but with long sideburns and horn-rimmed eyeglasses that accentuated amber eyes. He dressed in that metrosexual way that young men did, and Julie noticed Freddy eying him as his back was turned. She kicked him under the table and gave him a dirty look, which only made Freddy laugh.

"Marc, how long are you staying?" Freddy had asked, pursing his lips as he looked at Julie. She kicked him again.

"Oh, for two more days, then I visit with my girlfriend in Boston," Marc replied.

Julie's head dropped forward, as if her neck could no longer support its leaden weight.

"More wine, Jules?" Freddy lifted the bottle of red.

"Fill 'er up," she said.

***

Freddy fixed up the farmhouse in no time, and Julie was glad they'd decided to keep it for themselves and their business. It wasn't perfect, but the plumbing worked and the circuits were all now grounded. The last electrical system upgrade was in the mid-eighties, according to Freddy. Meanwhile, work began on the barn, and the weather was kind, allowing Freddy and his crew to accomplish things they normally wouldn't have been able to do in the winter. Rather than bring up men from New

York who would have to stay at the house during the week, he used his contacts to find able guys looking for work in the area, checked out their credentials and references, and hired them.

Valentine's Day was in a week. Freddy and the architect had split, amicably.

"I can't take weekends off to go into the city, and I don't have time for him if he comes up here," Freddy explained. "We're fine, and we both kind of knew this would be the case."

"Still," Julie mused. "Gilles."

"Gilles," Freddy agreed.

Julie wondered if she should plan a dinner party. She'd gotten to know a few other people in the area, and she could even invite Sarah and Zack, Ethan and Pauline up the road, if they didn't have other plans. A week was short notice, though. So she'd keep it all very informal, maybe an open house. Yes, an open house to show off Freddy's renovations. Maybe create some buzz around town for what was to come. She pulled on her jacket and ran across the yard to the barn, where she spotted Freddy along a far wall. She didn't enter the area, not without a hardhat, and she felt as though she were invading a foreign land. Besides, the guys were working. They were friendly, but distant. Hey, she wasn't trying to be one of them, anyway. And she was familiar with the standoffishness of the married man to the single woman. So she only ventured to the barn to offer coffee in the morning or cookies in the afternoon.

"Freddy! Got a second?"

Freddy walked toward her with long strides. He swiped his arm over his forehead, leaving dust on his brow. They stepped just outside the entryway of the barn. His hair was a tousled mess when he removed his hardhat.

"You here to help?" His face split into a wide grin.

"Not a chance, unless one of those guys wants to clean the bathrooms. What do you think of an informal open house next weekend? I know Valentine's Day is Sunday, but we could invite everyone we know, let them see how good the house looks? Maybe Saturday afternoon?"

"Next weekend? Valentine's Day? Jules, everyone but us probably has plans. Plans that don't include coming to see our property. How about I take you to dinner instead?"

"That's sweet, really, but I don't want to go out on Valentine's Day. The restaurants are all booked and you don't get good service. Plus we're not a couple. If you don't think it's a good idea…" She looked away, down the long gravel drive and up into the lonely hills.

"Tell you what. Let's do it at the end of the month, er, Sunday the twenty-eighth. It won't be tied in to hearts and cupids, and it'll give us a chance to plan. I'd like to invite some business people, too, folks who can help us promote the venue."

Julie brightened. That Freddy. "Great idea! If you want to wait until the first day of spring, we could do that, too."

Freddy squeezed her shoulders lightly and pressed his dusty lips to her forehead. "We'll talk tonight, babe. I gotta get back to work." He jogged back into the barn. Julie stood for a moment, watching him interact with the guys before heading back to the house. She needed some girlfriends.

He was right, of course. It was silly to think up a Valentine's Day party. But she would make an awesome dinner for him, since they were both alone right now.

***

Julie drove to the fancy grocery store in Pittsfield the following Saturday, armed with a shopping list for the entire meal. Beef Wellington tarts with haricots verts, which were really just extra-long string beans. She'd never made Beef Wellington before, but was excited to try it. She checked her list. Beef tenderloin. Cremini mushrooms. Frozen puff pastry. Foie gras mousse? The Price Chopper might not have foie gras mousse. She'd have known exactly where to go in New York, but Pittsfield wasn't Manhattan, and the Price Chopper wasn't Dean & Deluca. Okay, no problem, she told herself. Folding the grocery list and sliding it into her front pocket, she marched purposefully into the supermarket and yanked a cart from a long line of them at the entrance.

Thirty minutes later, she exited the market with three reusable grocery bags. No foie gras mousse. No cremini mushrooms. And no beef tenderloin. Instead, the ready-made foods section had tenderloin tips in gravy (four portions, in case Freddy wanted a second helping), garlic mashed potatoes, and green beans with bits of bacon. She bought extra of everything and all she had to do was warm up dinner in the oven. She even purchased a triple layer cake with chocolate frosting and raspberry filling. Who was she kidding, anyway? Freddy would be happy with this dinner, and she didn't chance ruining it.

It was cold enough to leave the groceries in the back of the car while she had her nails done in town, and she stopped for a bowl of chicken soup at the Misty Moonlight Diner before driving back home. She unloaded the groceries and placed dinner in the fridge. Plenty of time to soak in the tub and read some of her book.

She'd just settled into a bubbly bath when she heard the door slam.

"Jules! You here?" He called from the kitchen but she heard his boots approach.

"I'm taking a bath!" she yelled. There were still plenty of bubbles to cover her, so she added, "You can come in, though."

He pushed open the bathroom door and laughed. "Lady of leisure, I see!"

Julie fluttered her hands above the bubbles. "Hey, I was out all day, shopping for tonight's dinner. I'm just resting now."

"Okay, okay," he chuckled. "Well, I'm heading upstairs for a shower and a nap. I'm beat." He turned to leave.

"Dinner at six?"

"Sounds great, Valentine." She listened as he walked to the staircase, heard his steps on the stairs again as they faded away to his suite upstairs at the other end of the house. She knew he'd rather have had a date tonight. Well, so would she. But here they were, in western Massachusetts on Valentine's Day with no one but each other. Might as well make the best of it.

THOMAS

Thomas planned to take Maria to Vincent on Camelback for Valentine's Day dinner. His brother Don knew the manager and was able to secure a table for them.

"Bro, I'm glad you're making it work with this girl. She's a sweetheart, and Linda's happy you two are together. And trust me, it's good to keep Linda happy."

"You two okay?" Thomas asked.

"We are now. Couple of bumps in the road, but that's not unusual when you've been married as long as we have. Don't let the little things become big, Tom. Anyway, happy to see you with her."

Thomas knew he'd made amends with Don and Linda, but he wasn't with Maria for their benefit. He really cared for her, and wasn't about to screw up a good thing.

"Yeah, and thanks for pulling some strings to get this reservation," Thomas said. "She's thrilled we're going there, said it's one of the best restaurants in Phoenix."

"It is," Don replied. "This guy Vincent is great. He's a French chef who combines Southwestern ingredients into classic dishes. You're gonna love it, even if your wallet's hurting the next day." He paused. "So, how serious is this thing with you two?"

Thomas cleared his throat. "I love her, man. She could be the one for me. I mean, it's early, and I'm still earning her respect, but I'd do anything for Maria."

Don laughed on the other end. "About time, little brother," he said. "Well, the wife and I couldn't be happier to hear it. Don't waste time, either. She may be young, but you're not."

"Shut up," Thomas parried back. "Look, I'm not proposing tonight, so you can tell Linda not to get too excited. It's too soon. But…I don't know. I want to be with her, all the time." Thomas stared at the dancing flame of a candle, one given to him by Maria a few days ago. It smelled like cinnamon and reminded him of her.

"Alright then," Don said. "When you're ready to shop for a ring, let me know. I got a guy in the business."

"Of course you do," Thomas said with a laugh before hanging up. He sat in silence, watching the flame, thinking about his future. A future that included a slender, dark-haired beauty.

JULIE

Freddy complimented Julie on dinner twice, until she finally put up her hand to stop him. "I didn't make any of it," she confessed. "Price Chopper has a fabulous take-out section." She gazed lovingly at her forkful of mashed potatoes before sliding it between her lips.

"Come on," Freddy said. "You can cook! I mean, this stuff is great, but I thought you enjoyed making your own meals."

"I do," she said, setting down her fork to lift her wine glass. Freddy topped it off with the rest of the Cabernet. "I wanted to make Beef Wellington, but I should have tried the recipe first. And the supermarket in Pittsfield didn't have cremini mushrooms or foie gras mousse." She made a face. "Still getting used to life in the country, I guess."

"Well, this is excellent. And right now, I can't think of a better date than you." He paused to finish the wine in his glass and reached behind him for the second bottle. Holding it up in a silent question, he waited until she shrugged and nodded before uncorking it. "I'm not drinking this alone, Jules."

"Might as well, right? Misery loves wine." She gazed at Freddy through increasingly blurry eyes. "I need a man."

"I know you do, sweetie. So do I. Here's to finding them." He touched his glass to hers and drank.

***

Julie opened her eyes and closed them again. Darkness was preferable to the stabbing gray light that appeared at her window. Her head throbbed as if caught in a metal vise. And how did she forget to put on pajamas last night? Oh dear God, she thought. With her eyes still closed, she let her left hand slide across the mattress. Nothing. Whew. They'd have had to be pretty drunk to…come on, Julie, don't be an idiot. Still, how the heck did she end up naked?

She opened her eyes again, this time more accustomed to the flat morning light of winter. She listened. Silence, but she smelled coffee. Freddy must be up, but she usually heard him in the kitchen, humming or whistling or just walking around. She squinted at the little clock on the bedside table. 9:03! Yikes! She nearly jumped out of bed, then stopped herself. Why the rush? Coffee's on, the house isn't freezing cold for once. Still, she felt guilty. Julie wasn't one to loll around in bed all morning. There was always something to do.

She sat up and spied her clothes on the floor. Okay, so she was drunk last night, she peeled off her clothes and just crawled into bed. She definitely hadn't brushed her teeth. Ugh. Get up, she told herself, throwing back the covers and quilt just as Freddy tapped lightly on her bedroom door.

"Uh, hold on! I'm getting dressed!" she yelled. "One sec!" She tossed on an oversized sweatshirt, one that Tommy had left behind when he hightailed it to Arizona. She pulled up her black yoga pants and sprinted to the door.

"Morning!" she said in her perkiest whisper.

Freddy laughed out loud, too loud, she thought. "Good morning, sunshine," he said. "How you doing this morning? You okay?" He cocked his head and she wanted to wipe that smirky grin off his face.

"Fine, thanks," she muttered back. "Just let's keep the volume down this morning." Freddy backed up and she grabbed a pair of thick socks before following him out of her bedroom. Stopping in the dining room to cover her feet, she said, "I guess *you* don't have a hangover at all. How is that?"

"I didn't drink as much as you did, and I'm bigger than you are. Come on, I'll make you breakfast. Kale and beet smoothie? Wait, Jules, wait! I'm sorry," he called as she rushed to the bathroom and slammed the door behind her.

***

Later that evening, feeling clear-headed and avowing not to drink red wine for at least a week, Julie and Freddy sat down to a light supper of scrambled eggs and wheat toast and discussed the upcoming open house.

"This is our chance to introduce ourselves formally to the community, let them know we're here to stay, and get vendors interested in our wedding business," Freddy said.

Julie nodded in agreement, her mouth full of eggs. Once she had swallowed, she said, "Totally agree. But will the barn be ready?"

"Yeah, most of it. Definitely completed enough to hold a party. My guys are good; they've been working six days a week. We'll need a band, a caterer and staff…"

"Hang on, I need to make a list," Julie said.

"Already did. It's in the computer. I'll print it out if you want. Your job, if you care to take it, Miss Tate, is to design the invitations, figure out the guest list, and handle RSVPs. I'll coordinate with a caterer and find a good band."

"Nothing too loud, at least not in the beginning."

Freddy grinned. "Yes, ma'am. And I want to do some advertising. Remember my friend Alison who runs the PR agency? I think she might be able to help us out. We need to get some city people up here."

"I remember her. She's pretty high-end. Can she give us a break on the cost?"

He winked, and Julie knew he'd be using that Freddy charm. "I'll try, hon."

Julie sighed. "We'll check with each other on the numbers, though, right? Until we've got a client, all we've been doing is spending."

"I know, but she could get us some really good press. Maybe even a celebrity endorsement. These destination weddings are all the thing."

Julie gnawed on her bottom lip. "Yeah, but in Hawaii or Aruba. The Jingle Valley Farm in Dalton? In a barn?"

"That's why we need Alison! Let me get in touch with her, maybe even bring her up here."

"Okay. Do what you have to do." Julie rested her chin in her hand. She still felt the effects from all that wine the previous night and had downed over a quart of water since she'd gotten up. "I just hope we can make this work."

"Where's my optimist? Come on, Jules, you know we can do this. It's always sketchy in the beginning."

Julie nodded her assent. "You're right. Okay, let's get started tomorrow morning. I need to sleep tonight, a clear, non-wine-induced sleep."

"In your pajamas," Freddy said with a smirk.

Her head jerked up and she stared him down until he started staring at the ceiling. "How did you know that? How?"

He shook his head and laughed again. "You don't remember the best part? Julie, you called to me from your bedroom, said you had to show me something. When I came to your door, which was open, by the way, you were already naked and dancing around your bed."

"Oh good Lord," she moaned. She peeked up at him, only to see him looking back at her with kind and sympathetic eyes. "I'm such an idiot. A horny, pathetic idiot."

"Do you want to watch me shower tonight? Would that help?" He raised his hands, palms up.

"That would be absolute torture," Julie said with a small smile of her own. And before Freddy could respond, she stood up. "You've got the dishes tonight." And she left the room, pleased with herself.

THOMAS

"My parents are coming for a visit," Maria said. "They've never been up to Phoenix."

Thomas felt a contraction in his chest, but ignored it. By the time a woman talked about meeting her parents, Thomas was usually long gone from the relationship. This time was different, though, and he would get through it. They'd love him. He'd make sure of it.

"When?" Thomas wondered if he could get any time off. Golf season was year-round in Arizona, but he might be able to swing a day or two.

"First day of spring," she said. "I told them they could stay with me." She gave him a long look.

"Got it," Thomas chuckled. "We'll be chaste while they're here."

"Thank you. They're kind of old-fashioned, and I'm still their baby." She crossed her legs at the ankles and leaned back against his chest. "It's only a two-hour flight from El Paso, but my mom hates to fly."

"How long a drive?" Thomas asked, his nose buried in her hair.

"Oh, six or seven hours. Dad convinced her to get on a plane."

"What do your parents do?"

"My dad's an engineer and my mom teaches English as a second language in an Adult Ed program," she said, sitting forward and twisting to look at Thomas's face.

"Lots of Mexican-Americans want to speak English well, you know."

"You go back there often?"

She shook her head. "No. I feel kind of guilty about it, but there's not much there for me. I couldn't wait to leave when I was a teenager, that's why I applied to colleges in Arizona and New Mexico. You know, away but not so far away that there'd be tears," she said with a laugh.

There was still so much he didn't know about her, he realized. Was this thing between them moving too quickly? Would her parents think the same? They'd discussed some of the more important issues that couples deal with - both wanted at least one child but were open to as many as three, if possible; she was more of a saver than he was, but he had money in the bank, especially after Julie bought out his share of Jingle Valley; their political views meshed. Everything else could be figured out as they went along, right? And Thomas wasn't getting any younger. If they wanted to start a family, there was no reason to wait. He was thinking about a Christmas wedding.

"Are you listening to me?" She poked him in the side.

Thomas turned his eyes back to her pretty face. "Sorry, I was on a deserted island with you. And didn't you look fetching in that red bikini," he said.

"Come here," she whispered.

JULIE

It was just Jingle Valley now. No more 'farm.' That was the suggestion of Freddy's PR friend Alison, and Julie reluctantly agreed.

"We're not a farm, Jules, and we don't want to convey something that could turn folks off," Freddy said over coffee one morning.

"She's never even been here. Alison," Julie said, drawing out her name and making a face.

"Stop," he said kindly. "She's helping. She's taken over the marketing of this event, and used her considerable list of contacts to get some influential people interested in us."

"Yeah yeah yeah," Julie muttered.

"What? You should be thrilled about this, hon."

"So why don't we have more people coming? According to Al-i-son, the RSVP list is at forty-eight. And most of them are locals!"

"I know, but don't worry. I have faith in her, and I want you to focus on the catering and the music." Freddy ran his hand along the top of Julie's head as he left the kitchen, a gesture Julie found exceptionally annoying.

Sitting alone at the table, she refilled her mug. It was the money situation that had her on edge. Every day she logged into her account and watched it dwindle. She and Freddy had put up the same amount of money to get the business off the ground, and she was keenly aware that expenses were necessary to start up a venture like theirs, but she hated it.

She'd chosen a menu with the caterer that would (hopefully) satisfy everyone, but it was expensive, as was the quartet that would entertain the forty-eight attendees with light jazz throughout the evening. Light jazz! Did the good people of Dalton even want to listen to light jazz? Maybe she could call the guy and ask for standards instead – Sinatra, Mathis, Fitzgerald. Songs more easily recognizable.

She sighed heavily and listened to the muffled noise chainsaws and hammers. *Please let this work*, she implored silently.

Two days later a miracle occurred. Julie received an email from a woman named Margot Dexheimer, asking about the possibility of holding her wedding at Jingle Valley. *My fiancé and I are planning an October wedding, but I don't know if your venue will be up and running in time. Are you available for an onsite inspection this month?*

Julie stared at her computer screen as the reality sank in. A bride! A paying client!

After screaming the news to Freddy, she replied, inviting Margot Dexheimer to come, as their guest, the last weekend in March. Sure, the weather wouldn't be great, but they'd have the barn ready after the open house, and they'd be in a good position to tout the qualities of the space. They offered to put her up at the hotel in Pittsfield, but promised the honeymoon suite would be finished for her and her fiancé to view.

Margot confirmed the weekend, but said her mother would accompany her, not her fiancé.

"The guy has no say in this one, apparently," Freddy said when Julie told him the news.

"Not necessarily. Maybe he's too busy, or maybe he'd rather leave all the planning up to her."

"What's this girl's last name again?" Freddy asked, picking up his tablet.

"Dexheimer," Julie said, squinting at her laptop monitor.

He snapped his fingers. "I've heard that name, or seen it, before. Hang on." He typed something into the tablet and waited. "Yeah, there it is. She's loaded. Or I should say her family is." He handed the tablet to Julie.

"Really?" She stared at the screen in her hand. "Her father is Morton Dexheimer, CEO of Banister Black & Associates. What do they do? Oh wait, I see it. Hey, this guy owns half of Manhattan!"

"Well, probably not half, but he does own a lot of buildings in the city. I wonder if Alison suggested us to the Dexheimers. She has a lot of well-heeled clients."

"If she sent Margot to us, we need to thank her big time. I don't know how, but this is huge."

Freddy turned off his tablet and grabbed Julie's hand. "We need to figure out how much we're going to charge her. And I'm not saying that because I think we need to charge her extra, you know, because her dad is richer than God. But we can set the bar with her, and itemize our list of things a bride might want. Basic package price, plus add-ons."

"Right. But where do we begin?"

"I'll make some calls, ask around other places in the city, see what they would charge. Julie, depending on what she wants, this could be a gold mine for us."

"I just want to do a great job so she recommends us to her friends," Julie said. Seeing the look of Freddy's face, she added, "I'm excited, okay? I am! But she hasn't signed a contract with us yet. We still have a lot of work to do."

***

It rained on the first day of spring. Correction - it poured. All day. The ground around the barn was one big mud puddle, and there was a small leak in the roof that Freddy fixed before it caused any real damage. Julie called the party rental company and asked for anything that might shield her guests from the deluge, and fortunately, there was a portable awning, like the kind you see at New York apartment buildings, a covering that stretched from the barn entrance to the gravel driveway. Julie ordered it, and said she'd be by in the early afternoon to pick it up. She hung up the phone and cried, for the second time that morning.

"Stop raining! Stop it now!" she screamed at the window. The panes cried too, teardrops running down in rivulets, blurring everything outside that was soaked through.

"Hey," Freddy called as he descended the stairs. "Come on now, there's nothing we can do about the weather."

"It's going to ruin everything!" she wailed. "Look at the outside! It was bad enough there wasn't any grass yet, but this! The pigs will come back so they can wallow around in the mud."

"Julie, we never had any pigs," Freddy said gently.

"Well, pigs will find their way here for the glorious mud." She gripped her head with her hands, and when she let go, her hair stood out in different directions.

"Don't worry about it," Freddy said, draping a long arm over her shoulders. "These folks know what to do in bad weather. And you never know, the rain could end well before the party."

"Stop being such an optimist!" she said, pulling away from him. "I want pancakes." She opened a cupboard and pulled out a box of Bisquik.

"Here, let me do that," he said, nudging her aside. "You're dangerous in the kitchen when you're like this. You want chocolate chips in them?"

"What do you think?" she muttered, sinking into a chair and glaring out the window.

THOMAS

Francisco and Patricia Lopez's flight was scheduled to arrive at Phoenix's Sky Harbor airport at three o'clock in the afternoon, but Maria would stand alone in the arrivals section. Thomas had to work until six, but agreed to spend Sunday with 'the fam.' He'd told Maria it might be better for her to visit with her parents alone on Saturday evening, since he'd be grubby and tired from a long day at the golf course. She had agreed, and Thomas drove home from work, ready to savor a night to himself. Yes, he loved her, and he loved spending time with her, but everyone needs a little time away, right? That's what he told himself, anyway. Meeting the parents could wait a day.

He unlocked his door and entered his apartment, then set down the six-pack and phoned in his order for a large mushroom and pepperoni. Now that was a Saturday night. The Suns against the Rockets, hey now. His beloved Boston Bruins were playing the Florida Panthers, so he had options. He jumped in the shower for a quick rinse, excited about his 'guy night.'

MARIA

Four doors down, Francisco and Patricia watched as Maria stirred chili on the stove.

"Another *cervesa*, papa?" She eyed his empty beer glass.

"No, no, *cielito*. One is enough." He held up his hand and smiled at his youngest daughter.

"So, when do we meet this new man of yours? Thomas?" Patricia asked.

"Tomorrow. He worked today, a long day, and I told him to just go home and rest tonight. Tomorrow we'll spend the day together. Thomas and I would like to show you some of Phoenix's prettier places."

"You love him?"

Maria turned the heat off the stove and faced her mother. "Yes, I do," she said, nodding to both of her parents. "Very much. He's a good man."

"And he's from Phoenix?" her father inquired.

"No." She almost told them he'd only been here a few months, but stopped short. No need to tell them that. "He's from Massachusetts. He ran a farm there for years. Cows and chickens."

"Ah, an agriculturist! And he left the farm to move to Phoenix. But he doesn't farm here, does he?" Maria knew her parents were just curious, but all these questions! Maria poured beer into a glass, taking half and pouring the rest for her father. "No, he manages a golf course. He wanted to live in a warmer climate, that's why he moved to Phoenix." Thomas had answered all her questions early on in their relationship, about why he would leave behind land that he owned. He explained about Julie being part owner and buying him out. He told her all about his ex-wife and took most of the blame for the failed marriage.

"Well, that's very nice, sweetheart. And how old is he?" Patricia sat straight on the stool that Thomas always chose, and Maria wished for a moment that he was there to answer all these questions.

Maria turned back to the stove and ladled chili into the three deep bowls stacked up on the counter. "Thirty-six," she said quietly, hoping they'd hear it as twenty-six.

"Ten years older than you!" her father proclaimed. "And no previous marriage? No kids?"

Maria set the bowls in front of them, then pulled her own bar stool close to the counter, which served as a dining table, since she didn't have one. She put a huge dollop of sour cream on her chili, then added a few scallions. A bowl of shredded cheese was ignored.

"He was married before. No children. The marriage ended amicably." She avoided her mother's penetrating gaze.

"Ah," her father said, digging into the chili. "This is good, *cielito*. Very good."

She knew it was good. She was a good cook.

"Why did the marriage end, Maria?" her mother asked.

"Mama, Thomas and I have talked all about this, and I am satisfied with his explanation. But honestly, I don't think it should concern you if it doesn't concern me."

"Hmmpf."

"Patricia, leave it. Our Maria is a grown woman, capable of making her own decisions." Turning to his daughter, Francisco added, "We look forward to meeting him tomorrow."

Maria opened a bag of corn chips and grabbed a handful to put on her plate. Emotional eating, she told herself. Still the same, just like when she was a fat teenager. She carried most of her weight in her behind, but Thomas didn't seem to care. She smiled, recalling their last date.

"He makes you happy then, sweetheart?" Her mother rested a soft hand over hers, and Maria felt some of the tension in her shoulders subside.

"He does. Very happy." There had been no dates in high school, no boys calling on the telephone or knocking on the door. Her parents had tried to get a second cousin to escort her to her senior prom, but when she learned of it, she locked herself in her bedroom and refused to come out. She lost a lot of weight the summer before college, but didn't shed the lack of self-confidence that remained. Then there was Alfred, her "boyfriend" during sophomore year. Skillful and tender, she'd fallen hard for him. When Maria discovered he spent afternoons at the home of a wealthy married woman, she broke it off, and had herself tested immediately for an STD.

"And his last name? I don't think you ever told us," her father said as he scooped the last of the chili from his bowl with a large corn chip.

"Tate," Maria said, looking directly at her father. "T-A-T-E, Tate."

"Hmm."

JULIE

The rain did let up in time for Jingle Valley's big coming-out party, but the grounds were so saturated and muddy, any ideas of grounds tours were cancelled. Still, the guests who showed up seemed impressed with the renovated barn and its possibility as a party venue. With a capacity of two hundred guests, a spacious honeymoon suite attached to the back, a custom kitchen, and shuttle service to and from nearby hotels, Jingle Valley was truly a destination for discerning people. And it was gorgeous! Julie still marveled at the workmanship inside the barn.

Freddy's friend Alison showed up with her husband, a hedge fund manager who looked about twenty. And she had indeed put Margot Dexheimer in touch with them. During a rare quiet moment, Julie thanked Alison for the recommendation, and let her know that Margot and her mother were coming up to Dalton in two weeks.

"Oh, lovely," said Alison, an untouched glass of Prosecco in her tiny hand. "Margot is a bit high-maintenance," she added in a stage whisper. "I've only met her mother Emily once, but Morton is a peach." She tossed her head back and laughed, revealing a long white neck ringed with emeralds. "You'll have your work cut out for you, Julie, but believe me, if the wedding is a hit, Morton will drive loads of business your way, as will I." She patted Julie's arm before taking her young husband's elbow and leading him to the dance floor.

Julie made the rounds, shaking hands, kissing cheeks, and generally smiling until her face felt as if it would crack. She refrained from drinking any alcohol, and barely ate any food, but the rave reviews about the venue were enough to sustain her throughout the afternoon and into the evening. She caught Freddy's eye and tilted her head, a signal that perhaps this would be a good time to say a few words. He strode over to her, looking devastatingly handsome in his tuxedo.

"Darling," he crooned, holding out his hand to her.

"Dance later," she whispered. "We need to say a few words to the group."

"Of course," he said, still in Fred Astaire mode. "Shall we?" He offered her his elbow, and she took it as he escorted her to the dance floor, where a microphone stand stood front and center.

"Thank you all so much for coming to the debut of Jingle Valley!" Freddy was at ease in front of the microphone, and Julie wondered, not for the first time, why he chose a profession like construction when he was so well-suited to performance. "Julie and I couldn't be happier to welcome you here, and to show you what we've done with the place."

He paused as a smattering of applause spread amongst the attendees.

"We may have left Manhattan, but we can bring glitz and glamour to your event right here in Dalton."

Julie stepped in at that moment to finish their well-rehearsed speech. "And if you want a quieter, more rustic wedding, we can do that as well! Tonight you're seeing the barn in its ninety-eight-per-cent-finished state. We're already accepting reservations for summer weddings, graduation parties, and any other reason you can think of to kick up your heels and make some noise!"

Thomas pulled the microphone to his lips. "I think you've all had a tour, and seen the honeymoon suite, but if anyone hasn't, I'd be happy to escort you."

One woman yelled, "Take me, Freddy!" and everyone chuckled.

He pointed her out and blew her an exaggerated kiss. Julie saw that the woman in question was probably old enough to be his grandmother, but it was all in good fun. Freddy continued, thanking the many vendors who'd had a part in planning the event, especially the caterer and the band, and finished by telling everyone that the quartet, Fourever, would have everyone dancing for the next two hours.

He and Julie stepped off the stage and were immediately encircled by well-wishers. As the music swelled and the dance floor filled with couples, Julie edged away from the merrymaking. So many congratulatory exclamations and kind words, but no one had said yet that they'd be interested in booking the barn for their event. She knew they'd have to knock it out of the park with Margot Dexheimer if they wanted any chance of getting business from Manhattan.

THOMAS

Maria called Thomas early Sunday morning, after she'd told her parents she was going out for a morning run. She'd brewed strong coffee and set out fresh fruit and a chocolate cinnamon coffee cake for them, then grabbed her cell phone and headed into the hallway.

"Where are you?" Thomas asked.

"I'm right outside your door," she said with a laugh. The door to Thomas's apartment opened and he pulled her inside and into his arms.

"I missed you!" she said into his bare chest. God, she smelled good, Thomas thought.

"Everything okay with the folks?" he asked, holding her at arm's length to inspect her facial expression.

"Yeah, yeah, it's fine. I'm not used to guests. Well, except for you. No, it's fine. I told them I was going out for a run, so I need to be sweaty when I get back."

Thomas grinned. "I can arrange that," he said, pulling her close.

***

Thirty minutes later, after brushing her hair, a glowing Maria trekked back to her apartment and opened the door to find her parents standing side by side in front of her sliding-glass doors. They turned at the sound of her entrance.

"We were watching for you!" they said in unison. "Isn't that the running track out there?" her mother asked, pointing to the jogging path that circled the complex. A few joggers were out on this mild day, although Sunday mornings were usually pretty quiet.

"It is," Maria said quickly. "But…I decided to run on the other side this morning. There were more runners." She hated to lie to her parents. But what was she supposed to do, tell them she couldn't wait to see Thomas and they had a quickie?

"Anyway, I'm going to hop in the shower and get dressed. Thomas will be by in about an hour." She'd send him a text message.

"We're looking forward to meeting him!" her mother called after her.

When Thomas knocked on Maria's door an hour and twenty minutes later, he was met by a frowning Francisco.

"Hello." Thomas stuck out his hand and smiled tentatively.

Francisco looked down at it for a moment, then gripped it hard and squeezed. "We've been waiting for you," he said as he stepped to the side and allowed Thomas to enter.

Thomas walked into the familiar apartment, his eyes searching for Maria. Instead, he saw an older version of her standing in the small kitchen. This woman's dark hair was cut short, as he imagined Maria's would be in the future, after the babies. Whoa, Thomas! He shook his head slightly to stop his thoughts from running rampant, and focused on Maria's parents.

"Mrs. Lopez? Hello, I'm Thomas Tate." Again Thomas stuck out a hand, but this time the reaction was warm and inviting. Patricia took his hand in both of hers and clasped it.

"Thomas! We're so happy to meet you. You've met Francisco." She glanced at her husband, who stood with his hands in his pockets. "Maria? Thomas is here!"

And there she was. Thomas felt his heartbeat quicken at the sight of her, so pretty in a saffron-yellow sundress, her glossy hair pulled back from her face to fall in soft curls around her shoulders. She grinned at him, gleaming white teeth against luminous cappuccino skin. Thomas took three steps to her, kissed her chastely on the cheek for her parents' benefit, and whispered in her ear, "You're ravishing, you know."

"I know," she whispered back, taking his hand. "Thomas, my parents, Francisco and Patricia."

Thomas nodded to each, since he'd already shaken hands. Francisco eyed him warily and said nothing, leaving an awkward moment of silence that Patricia was gracious enough to break.

"So! Maria tells us that you've just recently moved to Phoenix."

"Well, the end of last year, yes. But I'm so comfortable here that it feels as if I've been a lifelong Arizonan. Or a Phoenician," he added, hoping it would draw a smile from Francisco. It did not. Thomas knew he'd have to work harder on the old man, but was grateful that Maria's mother seemed so welcoming.

"And you work at a golf course," Francisco said flatly. A statement from the engineer.

"I manage it, yes sir."

Silence again. Thomas squeezed Maria's hand then let it go.

"Shall we?" Maria picked up her purse and keys, and gestured toward the door. "I'll drive."

Thomas saw it. A raised eyebrow from Francisco to his wife. Why? Because Maria was driving? Thomas didn't care. Maria knew Phoenix better. And they weren't living in the fifties.

"Let's go."

JULIE

With the open house over, Julie and Freddy planned for the arrival of Margot Dexheimer and her mother. Julie spent three days over-cleaning the house, even though Mrs. Dexheimer had indicated that she and her daughter would stay at a hotel in Pittsfield.

"Look! I have no more nails, just chewed-down bits of keratin clinging to my fingertips," she lamented to Freddy.

"Come on now, babe. Stop with all the worrying."

"You're not nervous about this?"

Freddy raked his hand through his hair. "Look, the house looks great, the barn looks super, and the honeymoon suite is going to seal the deal." He opened the door to head outside. "I see Zack out there and I need to talk to him."

Sarah almost walked right into him.

"Whoa, Sarah! Didn't see you there!" Freddy sidestepped around her and disappeared. Sarah shut the door behind her.

"I made sourdough biscuits!" she said, offering a cloth-covered basket to Julie.

"Great," Julie mumbled. "I mean, thanks. Really, thank you. Can you just set them there next to the coffeemaker? Excuse me a second." She walked outside and approached Freddy, who was yelling at Zack. Sarah trailed behind her.

"The azaleas are too far apart," Freddy said, hands on his hips.

"Dude, what is your problem?"

"I want bursts of color, Zack. You planted them too far apart."

"I thought I could fill in the spots with annuals. Pansies, marigolds, then mums in the fall." Zack waited.

Freddy shook his head. "Fine, whatever. You're the landscaper. I don't care anymore." He stormed off, leaving Zack to stare after him. Julie watched Freddy walk around the back side of the barn, and, leaving Zack to finish planting, she walked around the side of the house, out of sight but close enough to hear Sarah complain to Zack.

"Man, I don't know what's up with Julie today. I made those biscuits because she said she liked sourdough. And I come outside to hear Freddy yelling at you."

Julie took a step closer to listen. She'd never been rude to Sarah before, and really, hadn't meant to be this time. She watched Zack, his hands in the dirt, look up at Sarah.

"We can't please either of them today, I guess." His dark hair hung over his face as he finished planting the last of the azaleas. He stood up, wiped his dirty hands on his jeans, and surveyed his work. "Nothing wrong with what I did," he said, just loud enough for Julie to hear.

"I think they're both nervous, and they need to find some love. Too much pent-up frustration there."

Julie's eyes widened. Was it that obvious?

Zack chuckled. "Well, let's leave them alone. They'll figure things out for themselves."

"But we care about them, Zack. I'm going to make eggplant parmesan. Freddy liked it last time, and it'll show them that we want them to be happy." Sarah twisted her hair around her hand.

"Alright." Zack draped an arm around Sarah's shoulders as they walked back to their cottage.

***

The arrival of Margot Dexheimer and her mother was not unexpected, was not delayed, and was not celebrated. Their train from New York arrived in Albany on time, and Julie was at the station, on the platform, waiting. She recognized them immediately – Margot with her Meryl Streep nose, the only thing about her that could be called thin, and her mom, an "X-ray," as Thomas Wolfe would have put it. Mrs. Dexheimer's fur coat glistened in the sun, and Margot's white rabbit (Julie assumed, with an inward grimace) jacket padded her large frame, doing absolutely nothing to flatter the girl. Julie surmised that Mrs. D. had little to say over the young woman's fashion choices.

She walked toward them with her hand outstretched. "Hello! I'm Julie Tate."

Margot rushed her, like a linebacker, grabbing her in a big bear hug. Julie's cheek was pressed against the fur vest (rabbit, she was certain).

"Let the poor woman go, Margot, she can't breathe," Mrs. Dexheimer said.

"I'm so excited!" Margot gushed, as Julie began to inhale again.

"We are, too. Welcome," Julie said, looking around. "Do you have luggage?"

Mrs. Dexheimer peered down the platform. "We each have a bag, dear. Check baggage claim. Come, Margot." The older woman walked with purpose to the covered escalator that transported passengers to the second floor of the recently refurbished building. Margot hurried along behind her, leaving Julie to figure out how to retrieve their luggage.

"Um, okay, I guess I'll go get your bags," she said in a small voice, hoping no one heard her, and turned back to the platform, seeking an assistant to tell her where the Dexheimers' bags might be. A uniformed man who appeared to be in a hurry pointed to the same escalator. So the bags were delivered inside the station? And what was she supposed to do, fetch and retrieve? Wow, Julie thought. This should be interesting.

Ten minutes later, Julie stowed the designer luggage in the car's trunk and slammed it shut. Mrs. Dexheimer stood at the passenger side and waited. Julie looked at her, and at Margot, who stood alongside her mother. Did they not know how to get into a car? Wait. Did they not know how to open a door? She walked around to their side and opened both doors. The women slid inside the back seat. Unreal, Julie thought. She slammed the doors and got behind the wheel, taxi driver for the stars.

Julie played the part of chauffeur for the hour and fifteen minutes it took to get to Dalton. Margot and her mother conversed with each other in low voices, making it clear that Julie was not invited to partake in their conversation. Twice she asked a question of the women, something innocuous like how was the train ride or had they ever been to this area before, and both times Mrs. Dexheimer replied with one-word answers – "fine" and "no." So she drove in silence. She didn't even turn on the radio, or play the Mozart CD, worried they wouldn't like it. She and Freddy needed this booking, and Julie would suck it all up for the chance at getting Mrs. D. to sign the contract.

"Would you like to see Jingle Valley first, or should I drop you off at your hotel and pick you up for dinner?"

"Oh, I want to see Jingle Valley, Mummy!" Margot chirped, and Julie glanced in the rearview mirror to see Mrs. Dexheimer nod her assent.

"Jingle Valley it is, then," Julie said.

They arrived and the back seat conversation ceased abruptly as Julie turned down the long dirt road that led to the former farm. Neither of the women said a word, and Julie kept looking in the rearview mirror to spot some kind of facial expression from either of them. Margot looked like a kid on Christmas morning, but Mrs. Dexheimer's face remained impassive. Julie pulled the car up to the front door and set the brake.

"Here we are!" she said brightly. She opened her door and stepped out, then remembered to open the back seat door. The women exited the car and stood, like statues, looking at the farmhouse, then at the barn.

Finally Margot broke the silence. "I love it!" she cried. "Viktor will love it, too." Julie saw Mrs. D. flinch at the mention of the fiancé's name.

"The house is where we live and work. Freddy and I," Julie said, waving a hand at the farmhouse. She thought it might be best to take them into the barn first. Where was Freddy, she wondered. He could charm the pants off both of them.

"You and Freddy live together?" Margot widened her eyes and licked her lips. She giggled like a twelve-year-old.

"Freddy and I are friends, and business partners. I live downstairs and he lives upstairs," Julie explained, casting a glance at Mrs. Dexheimer. She stood unblinking, wrapped in mink.

"Please, come this way." Julie started walking toward the barn, looking behind her to make sure the Dexheimer women were following.

"Surely you have more landscaping to do here," Mrs. D. said.

"Of course. Our gardener is currently planting a three-season landscape, although we won't see the spring bulbs until next April. The grounds will be alive in color this summer, and he'll fill in the gaps with annuals. Margot, you've chosen October, isn't that right?"

"Actually, I'm thinking about closer to Thanksgiving now. Will everything be brown then?" She stuck out her lower lip in a gesture Julie was sure she'd implemented since the time she understood that it could benefit her.

"That won't be a problem at all. In fact, the colors of autumn are so beautiful, we'll have plenty of orange and yellow and dark red. Those lovely purple cabbages? Do you like those?"

"I don't eat cabbage, actually," she said. "But you do what you want! Viktor loves November." She got a dreamy look on her face.

Julie opened the door to the barn and said a silent thank you that Freddy had put the heat on. She'd texted him from the train station and asked him to do it. But where the heck was he?

"Ooh, Mummy! Look!" Margot floated through the cavernous barn, touching wrought-iron wall sconces, fingering the table linens, tilting her head back to look upwards. It did look lovely, Julie thought.

Mrs. Dexheimer watched her daughter weave around the tables, touching things as she went.

"Ms. Tate…" she began.

"Julie, please, Mrs. Dexheimer. I'm Julie."

"Julie. And you may call me Emily. If you wish." Emily Dexheimer took Julie's elbow and steered her farther away from Margot, who was now halfway up the open staircase. "Wait for us, Margot!" she called, and her daughter waved back gleefully.

"Julie, neither my husband nor I are happy about this wedding. This, this Russian immigrant is not the man Morton and I would have chosen for our daughter. But she is smitten, and, well, her debut was six years ago. The chances of her finding a suitable mate now are quite diminished. Especially with all that weight." Emily's face twisted with thinly-veiled disgust.

"Margot is lovely," said Julie with as much sincerity as she could. "And if this man makes her happy…"

"He does," Emily said with a dramatic sigh. "And Morton has insisted that he sign an iron-clad pre-nup. I still think he only wants her money."

Julie began a slow walk to the far staircase, where Margot was now seated, texting.

"What does Viktor do, if I may ask?"

Emily made a soft noise, like a little thud, through her fine nose. "He works in his uncle's shop, some kind of business in Brighton Beach that supplies wheelchairs and the like to the elderly population." She lowered her voice to a nearly inaudible whisper as they neared the staircase. "God knows what goes on there."

Julie didn't have time to consider what Emily could mean. Margot stood and tugged on her skirt, which was painfully short.

"Are you ready to see the honeymoon suite?" Julie asked.

Margot clapped her hands and gave Julie a hug. "I'm so ready!" she exclaimed, causing her mother's hollow cheeks to pink. Emily looked away, as if she'd just seen a terrible accident.

Julie stepped in front of her and led the way upstairs. Freddy had built the kitchen at one end of the barn and the honeymoon suite at the other end. At the top of the stairway, Julie turned to the left and led the women down a softly-lighted hallway to the rooms Freddy and his crew had completed. She waited at the door while Margot caught her breath. Emily, on the other hand, appeared to be in a kind of trance.

"Here it is!" Julie pushed the double doors open with a flourish and took a few steps inside.

It really was pretty, she thought. Freddy had wanted to decorate the suite lavishly, insisting that a newly-married couple would appreciate the extra-special treatment. The good-sized sitting room had plush furniture and a large, flat screen television on the wall above a gas-powered, remote-controlled fireplace. There were wide windows with an expansive view of rolling hills to the south, including October Mountain in the distance.

"Wow!" Margot twirled around and nearly toppled over, catching herself on the arm of an overstuffed chair. "Mummy, I could live here forever!"

Emily clutched her mink to her body. Freddy hadn't turned up the heat in the suite, which was fine. No need to run it for just a few minutes, although it looked as though Margot would stay as long as she could.

Julie gestured to the opposite wall of the living room. "Here's a small kitchenette, just a fridge and a microwave." Opening one of the cupboards, she added, "We have glassware and plates, plus utensils, for midnight snacks."

"It's perfect," Margot gushed, ignorant of the stern look her mother leveled at her.

"Well, let me just show you the bedroom," Julie said, actually feeling a little sorry for Emily, who looked like a cornered cat. She pulled open French doors and stepped into the bedroom, which was as large as the living room. A king-size bed stood along the far wall, covered in a wedding-ring quilt Julie had picked up in Stockbridge. Colorful and fluffy pillows were lined up under a wrought-iron headboard. Julie wanted the flat oak headboard, but Freddy convinced her that newlyweds might want something…well, something to grab on to was how he had put it. Julie blushed at the memory.

"It's very well-appointed," Emily croaked, the first compliment she'd given since they entered the suite.

"Viktor and I are waiting until our wedding night," Margot said, batting her eyes. "He's such a gentleman! But really, Julie, I can't wait. I wish we were getting married today!"

TMI, TMI, Julie said to herself.

"Margot! That's quite enough," her mother admonished. Emily's voice was so sharp even Julie flinched. "Ms. Tate has no desire to hear about your private life. And neither do I."

"But Mummy, you were the one who said I should wait. You've been telling me that since I was twelve. I'm waiting, you should be happy." Margot crossed her arms, pushing her bosoms up to her neck. Julie had images in her head that she tried desperately to dispel. She thought perhaps it would be best not to show them the heart-shaped tub, the shower large enough for two.

"Well! Let's get you two back to your hotel so you have a chance to rest and freshen up." Julie led the way out of the honeymoon suite, anxious to ferry the

Dexheimers back to their hotel. It was already three-thirty, and she looked forward to a couple of hours without them.

"Julie, if you don't mind, I think Margot and I will stay in this evening, and spend the day with you and your partner tomorrow." Emily's voice was thin, and Julie thought she looked older than she had at the Albany train station.

"Are you sure, Emily? Is everything okay?" Margot twirled and hummed behind them, not a care in the world.

Emily took Julie's arm again as they headed down the staircase. "Yes, dear, and this is a lovely place. Thank you for the impromptu tour. Tomorrow you and I will sit down and figure everything out, but I'm a bit tired and could use a rest." She was really a tiny thing, wrapped in her fur coat.

"Of course. There's a restaurant next to the hotel. I apologize that Pittsfield doesn't offer fancier accommodations, but the hotel is clean and the restaurant is very good."

"That's just fine, dear." They were back in the main room of the barn, and Emily smiled as she looked around. A sad smile, though, Julie noticed. Of course. Emily had grander aspirations for her daughter, maybe a wedding at the Roosevelt Hotel, or Landmark on the Park. Julie had always dreamed of having her wedding at Le Bernardin, but she hadn't thought much about that lately. Still, in a family like the Dexheimers, with only one daughter to marry off, Julie imagined Mr. and Mrs. D.

were more than a little disappointed in their daughter's choice of a husband. But what are you going to do?

"I'll bring the car to you. Have a seat. I'll be just a minute." As she was exiting the barn, Freddy drove up in his truck. Tommy's truck. She waved and jogged over to him.

"Where have you been? I've had the Dexheimers here for the past hour!"

Freddy grimaced. "I was delayed, sorry. But I thought they were just coming in today, and we're meeting with them tomorrow?"

Julie continued talking as she headed to the car. She wanted to warm it up for poor Emily. "I thought so, too, but when I picked them up at the station, they wanted to see it all. Thanks for turning on the heat." She opened her car door. "Wait until you meet them tomorrow! But if I were you, I'd get in the house so they don't see you. I'll be back as soon as I drop them at the hotel. They're not eating with us tonight. Emily's tired."

"That's fine. I'm bushed. See you when you get back," he said, brushing his lips against her cheek.

***

The meeting with Emily Dexheimer went well, Julie and Freddy both agreed. The wedding was set for the first Saturday in November. Emily estimated two hundred guests, and Julie stated a price of one hundred fifteen dollars per person. Contracts were signed, and Emily left a check for the non-refundable deposit of five thousand dollars.

"We'll take care of the flowers and the music. But I will need contact information for a decent bakery to make a cake," she said. "Can you suggest anyone?"

"The Cakewalk makes gorgeous cakes," Julie replied, and Freddy agreed.

"Anita and Michael are wonderful people. I know you'll be pleased," he said. He flipped through a leather folder and found their business card.

"Thank you. I'll probably be back here in the summer, if that's convenient for you. That'll give me a chance to visit with the bakery and sample their cakes." She closed her eyes and Julie saw the corners of her mouth sag.

"It'll be lovely here in June, Emily," Julie said. "I know you'll be pleased with what we can offer to your daughter and her fiancé." She wondered if she should have asked for more of a deposit. There was so much riding on this wedding, and for a brief moment, Julie wished Margot would move up the date.

A gust of wind blew through as they stood outside, but Emily's hair never moved. Perfectly lacquered blonde helmet, that's what it was. Julie smiled.

"Morton and I are meeting Viktor's family next weekend. We've invited them to dinner at our apartment, and I'm dreading it." She let her gaze drift across to where Margot stood chatting with Sarah just a few feet away. Margot was animated, her hands flying everywhere, while Sarah stood still and nodded occasionally.

"I'm sure everything will be fine," Julie said.

"What are you serving?" Freddy asked. Leave it to Freddy, Julie thought. Emily's eyes brightened as she spoke with Freddy. He could melt ice in the Arctic.

"I spoke with my personal chef and told her to plan a simple, Eastern European-type menu. I don't know what these people eat, but I imagine they'd be comfortable with caviar and borscht. Morton wants steaks, so we're having steaks. Baked potatoes. Salad." She expelled a barky laugh.

"Sounds wonderful," Julie murmured, turning Freddy for confirmation as Margot bounded over to them.

"Are you talking about the dinner for Viktor's parents? Mummy, you should invite Julie and Freddy!" She swiveled her head from one to another.

Emily stiffened. "Margot, please. These people are very busy running their business." She turned to Freddy. "I apologize for my daughter's impetuousness."

Freddy held up his palm. "No worries," he chuckled. "Thanks, Margot, for the invite, but Julie and I really are very busy." He leaned toward her. "And we've got your wedding to plan!"

"That's right," Julie chimed. "Well, I should take you both back to the hotel so you can pick up your bags."

"Margot!" Emily called after the girl, and Julie was reminded of the collie they'd had on the farm when she was little.

THOMAS

Thomas had gone out of his way to show Maria's parents a nice time, he thought. Her father remained lukewarm, and just wasn't going to be happy with anything he did. If Francisco didn't think Thomas was good enough for his daughter, well, screw him. I'm going to propose to her and she's going to say yes, he told himself. Maybe they should elope and get married back east, he thought. He didn't want to go to El Paso for a wedding. El Paso! He'd have to convince Maria that a wedding would be better anywhere but there. Well, first he'd have to convince her to marry him. That was the very big first step.

The parents were in Phoenix until Thursday, but at least he had his job as an excuse to avoid them. He explained it to Maria.

"Honey, I was able to get away this weekend, but the boss can't let me off for the week. We're gearing up for the busy season, you know. And the weather's been great, so the course has to be ready to go."

"It's not like we had a harsh winter, though. Is there really so much that needs to be done?"

"Yeah," he said, as convincingly as he could. "I'll be there until six, easy. But I don't want you to hold dinner for me. I understand if your folks want to eat earlier."

She wrinkled her brow. He wanted to kiss her forehead, use his lips to smooth it out. "How about we have dinner together on Monday? I'll make something easy and we'll eat when you get home. Tuesday you take the evening off and relax. I'll take them to Sedona on

Tuesday and Saguaro in Tucson on Wednesday. Maybe Wednesday night we could go out to that pizza place you said you liked. I have to get them to the airport early on Thursday morning."

"So, Monday and Wednesday," he said, sticking his hands in his back pockets and rocking on his heels. "That's fine," he said while letting out a big breath, "but I can't wait until it's just you and me again. God, I've missed you." He wrapped his arms around her waist and pulled her in. He felt like a can of beer that had been shaken, but no one had popped the top yet. And heaven help her when she did.

***

Thomas acted like a grownup for the next few days, in spite of failed effort after failed effort to get Maria's father to engage with him on any subject. Thomas kept telling himself that it was Francisco who was missing out, and he didn't care, because the parents were flying back to El Paso and he would be alone with Maria. Then he realized how childish it all sounded. Come on, man, he chided himself, they're her parents, they love her, and she's devoted to them.

He wanted to propose on the first day of May.

A visit to see his brother Don the next day brought giddy yelps from Linda. Don had to calm her down for ten minutes.

"See? You had to move all the way out here to find the woman of your dreams. Five months, bro. You sure she's not gonna think it's too soon?"

"I feel pretty good about this," Thomas said, looking at both at them. Linda nodded like a bobble head doll, but Don leaned back in his chair and stuck his tongue inside his cheek so it bulged out.

"Look, we've talked about the important things, okay? We both want kids. We know each other's financial situation. Hell, I'm askin' her."

Don said, "We need to get Julie to move to Arizona now. Join the rest of the Tates out west. How is she, anyway?"

"Dunno," Thomas answered. "I haven't talked to her much lately. She and her friend Freddy are turning the farm into a wedding place. The barn, mostly. I keep asking her to send a picture." He shrugged. "Can't say it'll fly. Dalton's still in the middle of nowhere."

"I give her a lot of credit, though," Linda said, glancing at her husband. "She's trying to make it work, and it's something different than a tired old banquet hall or hotel. Where are you and Maria gonna get married – El Paso?" She winked and gave Thomas's shoulder a playful shove.

"I hope not. I'd like to convince her we should get married here, in Phoenix. Doesn't it make more sense?"

"Ha! Never gonna happen. 'Out in the West Texas town of El Paso...'" Don couldn't sing to save his life.

"Tommy, think about this," Linda started, pouring coffee for everyone. "What if you two got married at Jingle Valley? You'd be giving Julie the business, Maria could at least see where you grew up. It's beautiful country there, and Donny and me, we'd love a chance to go back."

Thomas snorted. "Ha. You two should go back then. Renew your vows. I left that place behind. Besides, Maria would never want to get married in Massachusetts."

Linda stirred her coffee but said nothing.

"What?"

"Nothing. I didn't say a word," Linda said, turning to face Don. "So, you two going ring shopping? Tommy, do you know what Maria wants?"

Thomas shrugged again. "A big rock, isn't that what every woman wants?"

Linda rolled her eyes. "Come on. You don't go and buy her a round diamond if she has her heart set on a pear-shaped. Or emerald cut. Or square. And what about the setting?" Seeing the look on Thomas's face, as if the point of a knife was edging closer to his jugular vein, she added, "Don, take him to see Boris. Tommy, let Boris know how much you can spend. Then you call him and let him know when you – and Maria – are coming in. Boris'll lay out a nice assortment of diamonds in your price range." She picked up her coffee mug and leaned back against the sofa. "That's how it's done."

Don looked at Thomas. "She's right, you know. Ready to go?"

JULIE

Julie attempted to do more walking. A brisk walk after breakfast, to energize her for the day ahead. Another walk after her day ended, but before it was dark. In the new day's fresh air, she came alive, almost running the entire loop around the property, waving at Zack, turning her face up to the sun, if there was any, or the rain. She savored the air, sharp and crisp, redolent of pine and earth. If she thought about it, she remembered the smells of New York – diesel and hot dogs and urine. And the quiet here! She woke up every morning to quiet. No garbage trucks rumbling outside her window, cars honking incessantly, jackhammers and their head-splitting noise. She thought she'd miss everything about the city, but she didn't.

The late day walks were different. Perhaps it was the more leisurely pace of afternoon, willing the daylight to last a few minutes more. Hoping to see a new face, the way she always did in the city on her way home from work. A handsome man who smiled first, or maybe she did, the unspoken words that two people could share without saying anything. The afternoon walks seemed to underscore her loneliness, but she wouldn't give them up. Maybe that was hope, she thought. Perhaps she should try a different route, although there wasn't much around town. And driving to Pittsfield to walk seemed absurd. Julie resolutely took three giant steps and rounded the corner by the church.

"Miss Tate!" a woman's voice reached her ears and Julie turned, trying to determine who owned it. She saw someone waving from across the church parking lot, so she waved back and walked in that direction. She didn't recognize the woman, who held the hand of a child, a girl of eight or nine, Julie guessed, dressed in a white karate uniform.

"Hi!" Julie said, hoping the woman would introduce herself. She smiled at the little girl, who grinned and showed two gaps where her teeth should be. Oh, she must be younger than eight, Julie thought. Don't kids lose those teeth around six or seven? She really didn't know these things. Then again, why would she?

"I know we've never officially met, but I knew your brother Thomas," the woman said, with a dreamy look on her face. "I'm Mary Jo Browning. He probably mentioned me to you."

"Oh, hi, Mary Jo," Julie stammered. No, Thomas had never mentioned her, or any other woman, for that matter, other than his ex-wife. Julie figured he had no love life, but then again, Thomas never had a problem attracting women. He'd been breaking hearts all over western Massachusetts since he was fourteen.

"So how is Thomas anyway? I couldn't believe it when he took off. I mean, we weren't dating or anything then. We decided to just stay friends, you know? I've got Taylor here to raise." She turned her head away from the girl to whisper to Julie. "I know your brother wasn't much for kids, and I understood. We had some laughs together, but I knew he wasn't the settling-down type." She smiled then, but Julie saw pain in Mary Jo's eyes, and could only imagine the letdown Tommy had given this woman. Typical Tommy. Love 'em and leave 'em. She prayed this little girl wasn't Tommy's, but then again, wouldn't Mary Jo have said something?

Julie cleared her throat. "We haven't had the chance to talk much lately. He's living near our brother in Arizona now, managing one of their many golf courses." Julie glanced at the little girl again. "You know, my business partner Freddy and I have turned the barn at Jingle Valley into a wonderful venue – for weddings, parties, bridal showers. We just booked a big wedding for the fall." Julie felt bad that Mary Jo hadn't been included on the open house guest list. "I'd love for you to come by some time and have a look, maybe stay for lunch?"

"I'd love to! Some day when Taylor's in school," she said, inclining her head to the girl, who nodded solemnly. "We do a lot of things together, but she knows that school comes first. Right, Tay? I tell her that the best asset a girl can have is an excellent education."

"Your mom's right," Julie said, thinking this little girl didn't look anything like Tommy. "Okay, then I'll call you. You can meet my partner, Freddy."

"Ooh! Partner as in partner?" Mary Jo gave an exaggerated wink.

"Business partner and friend," Julie replied coolly.

"Here, take out your phone. What's your number?" Julie recited hers as Mary Jo typed on the small device. "I just sent you a text that says 'MJ.' Now you have my number. I only use my cell these days." She smiled brightly at Julie. "Well, we should go, right Tay? I'm so glad we ran into each other!" She wrapped one arm around Julie while her other hand held Taylor's.

Julie remembered they didn't exactly run into each other, but whatever. "Me too, Mary Jo. I'll check my calendar and send you a few dates."

"See ya!" Mary Jo, with Taylor's hand glued to hers, turned and ambled back across the church parking lot.

Julie headed down the hill, in no hurry to return home. The sky was full of puffy clouds, the kind she associated more with a summer's day. According to the calendar, they weren't out of winter quite yet, but spring edged closer. She broke into a jog near the bottom of the hill and ran the half-mile back to Jingle Valley.

THOMAS

Thomas tried to imagine what Maria's idea of a romantic afternoon would be. He thought about hot-air ballooning, but fortunately remembered her fear of heights before booking the trip. What about the Desert Botanical Gardens? Nah, too crowded. He wanted to figure this one out on his own, not have to involve Don and especially not Linda. She'd write an engagement speech if he let her.

After some research, he decided to take her for a picnic at Fountain Hills, famous for its plume of water set in the middle of a thirty-acre lake. He scouted out the area and discovered a relatively private spot where they'd have a view, but wouldn't be distracted by all the people. He shopped for food - plump purple grapes (seedless, of course – no spitting), crusty bread and silky smooth Brie, roasted chicken that he cut into bite-size pieces (because it wasn't romantic to tear away flesh from bones), a box of imported chocolates, dark, the ones she preferred. A bottle of sparkling wine. No beer. Cloth napkins. A thick, soft blanket.

He checked the weather forecast. April was perfect and he'd finagled a Sunday off by switching with one of his co-workers.

JULIE

"I ran into a woman who dated my brother for a while. She's got a kid." Julie stirred a pot on the stove as Freddy set the table.

"His kid?"

"Oh! I'm sure it's not his. She didn't say, but…no. Anyway, I need to invite her to lunch."

"Why?"

"Because I told her I would," Julie said. She lowered the flame under the pot and opened the refrigerator to take out a stick of butter, setting it on the counter to soften. A knob of butter in the soup, the rest for the loaf of French bread warming in the oven. "Her name is Mary Jo. Freddy, it was kind of a big deal for me, just chatting it up with one of the locals and inviting her to lunch."

Freddy pulled out a chair and waited for her to sit before he seated himself. "It's fine with me. Just let me know when so I can be available. Is she a vendor? Can she do anything for us? This is lunch, right? Or do you want to have a dinner gathering, in which case I'd need to find a guy for her."

"Hell, Freddy, you and I can't even find dates for ourselves, I don't think we need to be matchmakers right now. I just wanted to invite her, you know, as a friend. I don't have any girlfriends." Julie pushed her chair back and checked the soup once more. She couldn't stay still. "We're good here. Hand me the bowls, would you?" She ladled thick, creamy soup into the two bowls, then pulled the loaf of bread from the oven, using a faded red potholder that she remembered her mom having when she was a kid. Amazing how some things withstood time. She placed the loaf on a big wooden board and set it on the table between them. Freddy sawed through the bread and tossed slices into a cloth-lined basket. Julie picked up the stick of butter, still wrapped in waxed paper, and tossed it on top of the warm bread.

"It's still cold," she said by way of explanation.

"No butter dish? We're slipping, Jules," he deadpanned. They really tried to make dinner an event. Julie was insistent; she feared they'd turn into a couple of slobs, eating from paper plates while slouched in front of the television, and even though she felt like doing that many nights, she forced herself to create a meal that they'd eat at the table in the kitchen, sometimes with Zack and Sarah. She even tried to look presentable. Even for Freddy, who couldn't look bad if he tried.

"Okay," she said, and reached for a milky-white ceramic butter dish from the cupboard next to the stove. They sat down to eat, New England clam chowder and buttered bread. "I should have made a salad," she said between mouthfuls. "We should eat salad more often."

"We will, when it's in season. This is fine." He ate hungrily, and Julie knew it probably wasn't enough for him. Still, she watched what she spent at the grocery store, and kept a careful eye on the household budget. With no income, there was no other option but to rein in spending. But she'd fight him for that last piece of bread if she had to.

"How about we have your friend to lunch next Thursday? I'll ask Zack to come with Sarah. Unless you were thinking just the two of you?"

Julie nodded and held up one finger while she chewed. "No, until I get to know her, I'm happy to have a few more around the table. Okay. We'll be five. If there weren't three of your guys working on the barn, I'd invite them all, but I can't. It's too much." She'd wanted to give them lunch in the early days, but realized it would be too expensive to add a meal for three to the cost of paying them. She and Freddy might not be drawing a salary, but his guys had to paid, every Friday.

"They eat just fine, don't worry about them."

"Yeah, their wives pack their lunches."

Freddy gave her a withering look before responding. "They're good guys, okay? I couldn't ask for a better crew. We should plan an event for when the barn is finally finished – just for them *and* their wives."

"You're right," Julie said tiredly. "But wouldn't it be nice if we both had dates for this special event?"

"Yes, my love. Hey, how come you didn't invite Mary Jo to the open house?"

"I didn't know her! I just met her, and she didn't show up on any of our lists. If she dated Tommy, she's probably familiar with the house." Julie gathered up the empty bowls and placed them in the deep sink before filling them with water. She'd get to them later. Here was another thing about her new life – dishes. She never cooked in Manhattan, never. No cooking meant no dirty dishes to wash. She made a mental note to pick up some of those yellow rubber gloves – her hands were always dry after washing dishes.

"What's going on with Tommy these days, anyway? Have you talked to him?"

Julie shook her head no. "No idea. He sends me these short, cryptic emails once a week or so. All I know is that he has a new apartment and a job at a golf course. He really left all of this behind when he moved out west. You know, Freddy, in some ways it's like he was never here. Meanwhile, you and I are building our business, and right now everything hinges on the Dexheimer wedding." She picked up a cotton dish towel from a wooden peg next to the sink and wiped her hands. "Everything. Because right now she's all we've got." With those words, those leaden words, Julie sagged. Her entire body slumped against the kitchen counter.

Freddy slid up behind her and began massaging her shoulders. "Everything's going to be fine, Jules. You'll see. Their wedding will be fairy-tale perfect. It'll put us on the map, and drive business to us." His words were like balm, his voice hypnotic. "You'll see, honey. We'll be so busy you'll have to hire a young man to massage your tired aching body."

Julie rolled her shoulders under his strong kneading. "I think the wedding will be good, but it's over six months away and we have nothing else on the calendar. I was really hoping we'd get a graduation party, or a retirement, or something after the open house. All we got was one phone call, from Margaret Pother. She wanted to know if we could accommodate her book club. All eleven of them. Plus she wanted a discount! Said I should give her one."

"Why?"

"Because she used to buy eggs from my parents! Can you believe it? I tried to negotiate something, you know, offer a streamlined menu, that sort of thing, but she said we were too expensive and they could just meet at one of the women's houses. Freddy, we can't lower our prices any more than we have. A book club!"

Freddy continued to press his thumbs into her knotted-up muscles. "And we won't. Julie. We're a quality operation. Listen, we may not be for the locals, or maybe not until they hear about the kind of party we can throw here. It's the New York business that's going to put us on the map. I know you hate waiting until November for the wedding, but we can do some advertising now, in anticipation. After all, Mrs. Dexheimer gave us a deposit, she signed the contract. I'll call Alison and see what we can do to promote the event – and promote us." He removed his hands and turned her around. "Better?"

"Better." She leaned against his chest and he wrapped his long arms around her. Pressed against his body, warm and safe, she blinked back tears. In spite of all her self-doubt and worry, here with Freddy everything was good. "I need a man, Freddy. You know I love you to bits, but I need a man."

His loud laugh startled her. "What's so funny about that?" she asked, pulling back.

"Nothing! I know you do, babe. You need it bad. We'll work on that tomorrow, okay?" His eyes were shiny with teasing, but Julie knew how much he cared.

***

The telephone rang late on a Friday morning. It must be a supplier, Julie thought. Friends always called her on her cell. She picked up the receiver. "Good morning, Jingle Valley."

"Jules, it's me, Tommy."

She hesitated. They hadn't spoken for weeks, and she had little idea what was going on in his life. Meanwhile, she was checking her bank balance online daily, watching the funds she and Freddy had earmarked for their business drift out like the tide. Hearing her brother's voice caught her off-guard, and she felt a pull on her heart, a submerged longing for her family.

"Hey," she said slowly. "What's going on?"

She heard him take a deep breath, which could only mean bad news. Don? Eric? Eric was a heart attack waiting to happen, according to Tommy. Was he coming back to Jingle Valley? Tired of Arizona already? Typical Tommy, he couldn't stick with anything.

"I'm engaged! Getting married! Can you believe it?" His voice sang through the line, right into her ear like ragged fingernails being dragged slowly down an old chalkboard.

"What?" She swiveled her chair away from her computer monitor, away from her bank's online statement and all its terrible meaning. "Married? Really?"

Her lungs felt smaller, as if they were shrinking inside her chest. She stood, and sat down again, hard.

"I know, right? Last one you'd expect! Hell, Jules, I was sure you'd beat me to the altar. But Maria – well, you'll see when you meet her. You're gonna love her, Jules. We thought we'd take a trip out east. I want to show her the place, you know, where we grew up. Show her the farm and everything."

Coming east. And engaged. Show her the farm, only there's really no more farm. Hadn't she told him? Boom! Something fired up the synapses in her brain. "Congratulations! Can't wait to meet her. And to see you, it's been too long. So, when's the wedding? Have you set a date?" *Please say you'll consider Jingle Valley. Pleasepleaseplease.*

"She likes late summer, early fall. Her folks are from El Paso, and she's got a big family, so I know they want to do a big wedding down there…" Julie held her breath. "But she doesn't really want a big wedding. Something simple, you know? But in a church. Has to be in a church. Which means I'm now attending mass with her on Sunday mornings. Me! Ha! Jules, I'm really happy. Moving out west was the best decision I could have made."

Julie started talking before she could even form her thoughts. "Tommy, I'm so happy. Really, really happy. And if El Paso and a big wedding aren't for the two of you, come for a visit and let me show you what we've done with the place. Oh, you'll still recognize it, it hasn't changed that much. Well, except for the cows and the chickens, 'cause we don't have them anymore, but the barn, Tommy! Wait 'til you see the barn! You'll love it. And if it looks like the kind of place where you'd like to have a wedding reception, nothing would make me happier than to host your wedding here at Jingle Valley. You know, after the church ceremony." She stopped to breathe, realizing she'd been running her mouth off.

Thomas laughed. "You got it, sis. So, how's next week looking for you?"

***

She couldn't wait to relay the news to Freddy. He was in Manhattan for the day, meeting up with his friend Alison, and probably just sitting down to lunch. She texted him anyway, even though she figured he'd have turned off his phone.

Two hours later, he called as he was about to board the train back to Albany.

"Hi doll, what's this great news?"

"Freddy, you're not going to believe it. Tommy got engaged! To a girl in Arizona. And they're coming for a visit next week. I think we might be able to convince them to have their wedding reception here!"

"No shit. Tommy getting re-married. Never thought I'd hear or say those words in that order," he chuckled. "When's the wedding?"

"Not sure. She wants late summer, early fall. We could do it, with the Dexheimer wedding in November. And Freddy, we could really use the money," she added in a whisper, even though no one else was in the house.

"I know," he said. "My lunch with Alison netted a few ideas. We'll talk at home, okay?"

"Okay. See you soon."

THOMAS

"Well, I'm all for a visit east, Thomas, but I don't know about a wedding there. My entire family lives in Texas, New Mexico, and Arizona. That would be a huge expense for them to travel to Massachusetts." Maria mashed avocado in a wooden bowl, pressing a fork into the soft green pulp. There would be no chunks in this guacamole. Thomas watched her hands, the sparkle of her diamond engagement ring a brilliant distraction.

"Well...we could always have two weddings," he suggested. She looked up sharply and he hurried to explain. "I mean, we could have a small wedding back on the farm, something simple, just a few guests, people I knew there, and another event in El Paso after we return. A big party for all of your relatives!"

She stared at him for a good twenty seconds, and he shifted in his chair, waiting for her to say something.

"Or we could have a real wedding in El Paso with my family, and then a party in Massachusetts with yours." The thinnest of smiles appeared on her lips as she returned to making guacamole.

"Sure. So, how about we fly up there next week? We could leave on Friday, fly back Sunday night. I really can't get any more time off. Weekends are busy for me, but I got Hank to cover my shifts. I just have to work for two weeks straight when we get back."

Maria set the fork down in the bowl and pushed it off to the side. "Thomas, things are moving quickly. It's a lot for you. In the past few months you've relocated across the country, started a new job, and now we're engaged. I just want you to promise me you'll talk to me if you start to feel overwhelmed by all of it. Will you?"

"Yeah. Of course," he said casually, dipping a large corn chip into a bowl of salsa and stuffing the entire chip in his mouth. He held up a hand while he crunched and swallowed, then grabbed his beer and took a swig. "Maria, honey, I want to be married to you. If we could get married tonight, I'd find a way to do it." He took her hand in his. "We can have a regular church wedding in El Paso, in front of your family, and a big ol' party in Massachusetts. Would that make you happy?"

She nodded so vigorously he had to lay his big hand on top of her head.

***

Thomas and Maria's flight arrived at Hartford's Bradley Airport, which was a ninety-minute drive each way from and to Jingle Valley. Freddy insisted on driving, and Julie was happy for the company.

"I wish he'd have flown into Albany, though," Julie muttered as they pulled away from a Dunkin' Donuts off the Mass Turnpike.

"Pretty much the same distance, Jules. I checked. It seems like a shorter ride to Albany, but it's really no different."

"And he never thought to rent a car, apparently."

"Hey, what's the matter? Aren't you happy to see your brother again? Come on, Julie. Rant to me, okay, but you gotta turn on the nice for Thomas and his fiancée."

"I know," she said, looking out the passenger window. "I know. I just hope he likes what we've done to the place."

"Well, I hope so, too, but if he doesn't like it, so what? He doesn't own it anymore, Julie. You bought him out. This is something we've done together, and I'm damn proud of what the old farm looks like now."

She sat up a little straighter and set her Styrofoam cup in a holder between them. "You're right. And if he doesn't want to have a wedding there, well, whatever. I'm not giving it to them for free, though. We can't afford it."

"I'm sure he wouldn't expect to rent it for free." Julie snorted her reply. Freddy squeezed her knee. "Honey, take a deep breath." He glanced over at her. "And, yeah, we need to find you a man. Sorry it didn't work out with Chuck. He seemed interested when I talked to him about you."

She dismissed his comment with a hand wave. "He's a jerk. And I am *not* old enough to be his mother. What is he, eleven? Leave it to Zack and Sarah to fix me up with a college kid."

Freddy chuckled and maneuvered into the passing lane to pull ahead of a rusty old minivan. Julie turned to look at the driver as they passed and the grizzled old guy in a ball cap wiggled his tongue out at her. And not the way a seven-year-old would, either. She recoiled at the sight.

"Well, we'll find you someone. Then we'll find one for me. But ladies first."

"I love you, Freddy."

"Love you, too, sweet."

***

"I know it's dark out, and you'll see everything better in the morning," Freddy said, picking up Maria's bag. "But we put you two in the honeymoon suite. This way you can really see if you like it."

Julie took Thomas's arm. "We'll let you get settled in upstairs, then come back to the house for dinner."

"You sure we can't take you two out tonight? Jacob's Pub? The Mill Town?" Thomas picked up his own bag and gestured for Maria and Julie to precede him up the stairs. The women hadn't stopped chatting and laughing since they'd met.

"No, Tommy, I cooked. And you're probably tired from the flight. We can go out tomorrow night," Julie said. She turned at the top of the stairs and saw her brother shrug as he glanced at Maria.

Freddy opened the doors to the suite and stepped in. He reached for Thomas's bag with his free hand and disappeared into the bedroom to set down the luggage.

Thomas stood in the middle of the living area and looked around. His jaw went slack and Julie wanted to jump up and down with glee. He had no idea what they'd done to the place, but he had made a few pointed remarks on the drive from the airport about them selling off all the animals. Now Julie waited for what her brother had to say.

"Wow," he said in a low voice. "Fred, you did all this?"

"My crew and I did, yeah. You like it?" Thomas nodded slowly, taking it all in. "Well, come see the rest of it, then," Freddy said, leading the way into the bedroom.

"Oh!" Maria's hands flew to her cheeks. "*Que linda!* So pretty."

Thomas put his arm around Maria, seeing her obvious delight. "Sure is. Really nice, guys."

He looked at Julie and grinned. "You did it, Jules. You and Fred, you transformed this tired old farm into something special. Congratulations."

"We're really glad you both like it," she said, then turned to Freddy. "I'm heading back to the house to get dinner ready. You two come over anytime." With a slight incline of her head to Freddy, she turned to leave.

Once they were gone, Thomas picked up Maria and swung her around the room, then laid her gently on the quilt-covered bed. "Honeymoon suite," he whispered, running a finger along her perfect jaw and down her exquisite neck.

JULIE

During dinner, Thomas and Maria talked about how they met and where they got engaged. The more Julie knew about Maria, the more she liked her, and the more certain she was that Maria was perfect for her brother. She just hoped Tommy appreciated her.

"The asparagus is from our vegetable garden," Freddy said. "Well, Zack maintains it."

"They're great, huh?" Thomas said, pushing his carrots around on his plate. "I'll have to be sure to see them tomorrow."

"Thank you for making fish," Maria said. "We don't have it so much in Phoenix, unless it's fish tacos."

"Well, we're not on the coast, but we do have access to fresh scrod and lobster," Julie said as she pushed rice pilaf onto her fork with her knife. "I thought about serving lobster, but wasn't sure you'd like it," she added to Maria.

"So, what we were thinking was to have a family wedding in El Paso, then a couple of weeks later, come up here for a reception, a barn party." Thomas wiped his mouth and laid his linen napkin over his carrots.

"That's a good idea. You've got plenty of friends around here, Tommy," Julie said. "I'm sure you could fill the barn."

"Well, we want to keep it simple, but you're right, can't leave anyone out."

"Dinner was delicious, Julie," Maria said, arranging her silverware on a clean plate. "Thomas eats so much Southwest and Mexican food now, I'm sure he misses a real New England meal."

Thomas gazed at his fiancée with gooey eyes, and Julie stared at her brother, a smile on her lips. She almost made a snide remark – after all, this was Tommy – but held her tongue. If he'd reinvented himself to please Maria, who was she to ruin it? "Maria makes the best guacamole," he groaned.

"We could do a Mexican-themed party if you'd like," Julie offered, ignoring Freddy's pleading look that said not now, please, Julie.

Maria shook her head. "We'll have that in El Paso," she said. "I think it would be nice to have something that reflects the area. Right, honey?"

"Anything you want, baby," Thomas murmured, and Julie gulped down her wine.

***

Maria asked Julie to set aside the last weekend in September for the reception.

"El Paso in August is hot! Thomas will kill me later," she said with a laugh. "Thank you for doing this, Julie. We're both very grateful, and I know Thomas is thrilled to have our second wedding party here, on his farm." Julie wondered if Thomas had told Maria that it was no longer his farm.

"It's our pleasure! You know, when Freddy and I took over, we had some big ideas. I was determined to keep Jingle Valley in the family, especially since I'm the only one left living on the east coast. It's taken us a lot of work – well, especially Freddy and his crew – to transform the barn." Julie hesitated. Should she discuss the costs with Tommy? Or with them both? She laid her hand over Maria's, a gesture of sisterly solidarity. "Should we talk particulars, or wait for Tommy to join us?"

"Let's wait for Thomas," Maria said. "We're planning our wedding together, and I want him to have a say in everything. I never wanted to be one of those brides who didn't include the groom in the decisions! And Julie, thank you again for this beautiful gift."

Gift? Uh-oh, Julie thought. She'd better grab her brother fast.

***

"Hey, you." Thomas walked right into her bedroom without knocking. Julie fluffed the pillows on her bed and whirled around, a smile fixed on her face.

"Hey! Come on in, I wanted to talk to you." Thomas sat heavily on her bed and looked up expectantly.

Julie lowered herself to sit beside him. "I'm so happy for you two!" She ran her tongue over her teeth and felt the pinpricks of sweat begin on the back of her neck. Say it, she commanded herself.

"Tommy, we can give you a huge discount for the wedding reception. But we should talk numbers, and what you're willing to spend." She forced herself to look up and into his eyes.

"Oh! Oh, I thought…wait, why did I think this was like your wedding gift to us? Didn't you say come to Jingle Valley for the wedding?"

"I did. I'm thrilled you two would have a reception here after your El Paso wedding, but Tommy, this is our business. We can't give it all away."

Thomas sat quietly, his jaw set. Julie knew the look. It took him a minute to respond.

"Right. So, this would be your first big event?"

Julie nodded.

"So, the money you paid me when you bought me out of the place, I just turn around and give it back." He gave a short, hard laugh.

"Come on, Tommy. It's a fraction of what you were paid for the place." She stood and spread her hands, palms up. Think, Julie. Offer something he can live with. But don't let on how desperate you are. "We can let you have the place for half off. You pay for the bar bill. We'll work out the menu so that you and Maria are happy, and I'll spring for the flowers – my wedding gift to you." She wanted to kick herself. She should have treated him like any other customer.

"You're a crummy negotiator, you know that?" Thomas stood and stretched out his hand. "Deal, little sister."

Julie took his hand. "You're paying for the music," she added.

***

Julie spent the rest of the spring planning two weddings – the Lopez-Tate and the Dexheimer-Polzin nuptials. She was so busy she had no time for meeting anyone, but that didn't stop Freddy from trying. On a Saturday evening that was warmer than normal, they drove an hour to Easthampton to listen to a jazz trio and a swing quintet. As soon as Freddy left their table to use the restroom, a stranger sat in his chair.

"Sorry, this seat's taken," Julie said.

"I know. I just wanted a chance to say hello. Is he your boyfriend?"

That happened a lot. Julie smiled. "No, just a friend." She looked at the stranger's face. He was cute. Scruffy but clean. Nice smile and pretty eyes. "I'm Julie."

"Noah." He offered his hand. The band started up, an old song Julie remembered. One her parents liked. "Dance?"

Julie glanced around the room for Freddy and spied him chatting up a guy at the bar. "Sure."

In other words, darling, kiss me.

They danced close, very close. Julie could smell him, feel him, and it had been such a long time. This was nice. It was better than nice, it was wonderful. Right up to the moment his wife stormed in.

"Douglas!" *Douglas*? "Figures. Your sister said you'd be here. Bowling night, my ass!" She pulled him away and glared at Julie. "So you're the one." Her eyes blazed with savage fire.

"I'm no one! I don't even live around here! Freddy!" Julie bellowed his name and he came running. "You're a real jerk, you know that?" She pointed to Douglas/Noah, who looked a lot less attractive with a scary wife standing next to him.

"Don't you call my husband a jerk!"

"Okay, we're outta here," Freddy said, taking Julie's arm and trotting her to the door.

On the dark and starless drive back to Dalton, she wiped her cheeks. "I give up. It's not worth it."

"Stop that. He was a loser, Jules. There are good guys out there."

Julie slumped in her seat. "The good ones are all gay," she grumbled.

Freddy sighed heavily and drove on.

***

At the end of June, Julie received a surprise email from her former assistant Harmony. They'd exchanged messages in the early weeks after Julie had left New York, but the emails became more sporadic and finally stopped in May. She read Harmony's message with interest.

Hi Julie – Sorry I haven't written for so long. I just didn't feel like writing about my miserable life when everything is going so well for you. I'm happy for you! And I would love to come up for a visit. Hubs says he'll watch the kids if I come up for a weekend – what do you think? If you're too busy, I understand. Lots of stuff going on at work – I'll tell you in person. Let me know if I can come up, okay? Miss you lots.

What was going on at work, she wondered. And did she care? Not really, although she thought about her old job every time she checked her bank account balance online. Julie and Freddy had vowed not to touch their respective retirement accounts, but every month she worried more. Maybe having Harmony come to visit would be good for her. She typed a quick reply.

How about the weekend after the Fourth? Take the train to Albany and I'll pick you up. Call me when you have a plan. Xx

***

Harmony's visit was just what Julie needed. Their work relationship had always been comfortable, but now that Julie was no longer her boss, they were more like sisters. Harmony had met Freddy once, and they got on well. She and Sarah, however, seemed to be more like two magnetic poles that repelled each other. The two women couldn't have been more different, so maybe that was why. Harmony wouldn't be seen in public without lipstick and mascara, and her clothes, even her casual clothes, were impeccable. Sarah was comfortable with no makeup, no hair products, and no fashion sense. Julie had to admire each of them for their self-confidence.

Julie learned that Harmony had become close to Kendra, Maxwell's assistant, since they took lunch together nearly every day. Maxwell was not pleased with Candace Russell, Julie's replacement, and Kendra had whispered to Harmony that Candace's job was on the line. Meanwhile, there had been layoffs during the first months of the new year.

"If you wanted to come back, I bet he'd be happy, Julie. I'm just saying." They sat in their pajamas, drinking diet Coke and eating peanut M&Ms. The television upstairs in Freddy's room provided a low, unintelligible background noise.

"Oh, I can't go back." Julie shook her head for emphasis, or to convince herself of her statement. Her apartment was sublet, her life was here now. But that salary would sure be nice.

"Well, I miss you a lot. Everyone does. Candy – sorry, Candace – is bitchy."

Julie hugged her friend. "Come on, let's watch a movie. There's nothing else to do around here." Which is okay, Julie reminded herself. This is what I chose, and I want to make it work. We'll be okay. One way or another, we'll be okay. There are two weddings coming up, and the money will start flowing in. Out of Harmony's peripheral vision, Julie crossed her fingers.

THOMAS

Julie's cell phone rang Sunday afternoon. She'd just said goodbye to Harmony at the train station. It was Thomas.

"Hey, Tommy. How's everything?"

"Not good, Jules. Listen, I have bad news. Maria's mom had a stroke last night. She's alive, but it doesn't look good at all, at least not according to Maria's brother. We're heading to El Paso now."

Julie's thoughts were everywhere as she sat in her car. Maria's mother. A hospital bed. Her own mother, so sick at the end. Holding her hand. The wedding. But she dared not ask about the wedding. It would be so crass. As it turned out, she didn't need to ask.

"Jules, about the wedding and everything. It's all on hold for right now, until we see how her mom is going to pull through. But I wouldn't count on us coming up. Maria, she can't think of anything right now, and a wedding is about the last thing on her mind. I'll call you when I know more."

"Of course. I understand, Tommy." She did understand. No one could think about such a joyous occasion at this time. Still, it was about the only thing on Julie's mind during the long drive home.

***

The only news she had from Thomas was cryptic. "Will call soon." When she typed a message back asking about Maria's mother, another terse reply: "Soon."

Julie focused everything on Margot Dexheimer and her fiancé. Emily Dexheimer had a long black car drive her up to Dalton in mid-July, and she arrived alone. She'd wanted to come up sooner, but mentioned something about too many social events crowding her calendar.

Julie arranged for visits to The Cakewalk and Millie's Flower Cottage while Emily was in town. Sarah had expressed a desire to create the wedding cake, especially after taking a cake-making and decorating class, but Julie felt it was too important not to trust a professional. Instead, she asked Sarah to make cupcakes for the next-morning brunch, and a small, special dessert to leave for the couple in the honeymoon suite.

At The Cakewalk, Emily took small bites of lemon raspberry, carrot, and mocha cream cakes. Julie sipped coffee, vowing only to taste if Emily asked.

"The lemon raspberry is delightful, but with a November wedding…" she shook her head. "The carrot is probably more suitable."

"Whatever you think Margot would like," Julie murmured.

"Hmmph. Carrot." Emily set her fork on the small plate and leaned forward slightly. "We're having a dress made for her. I brought in a nutritionist to help her with her late-night binges. Maybe she could lose a little weight before the wedding, but she insists this Viktor likes her just the way she is."

What do you say to that? Julie bought a few seconds by finishing her coffee. "Margot is a beautiful young woman, Emily. And I know for certain she'll be a lovely bride."

Emily eyed her. "All right. You've made your point. Let's go to the florist."

***

Millie McNiff was hunched over an arrangement of pink roses and Gerbera daisies when Julie and Emily entered the shop. She stuck two pink tulips into the center of the arrangement and looked up.

"What do you think?" she asked. "Oh, Julie! Hello, dear." She held up the pink bouquet. "Becky Jordan had a little girl this morning. You remember Becky?"

Julie shook her head and glanced at Emily, who stood waiting.

"Oh, she's probably younger than you, honey. She's about twenty-four." She set the flower arrangement back on her work counter.

"Millie, let me introduce Emily Dexheimer. Mrs. Dexheimer's daughter will be getting married at Jingle Valley this fall and we'd like to talk with you about flowers for the event."

"How do," Millie said, offering a hand. Emily looked at it before taking Millie's fingers. "Now, when is this wedding?"

"November the fifth," Emily replied. Her skin was so taut that there could have been a ventriloquist saying the words. Julie barely saw Emily's lips move.

"Ooh, November," she said, clucking her tongue. "That's okay, we can work with it." She glanced at Julie. "Of course I'll be retired by then."

"What?? Millie, you can't retire!"

"Oh, not to worry, sweetie. My nephew Luke is going to take over for me. He'll be coming down in October. That's my Luke in this photograph." She picked up a framed photograph of a good-looking man laughing at the camera and held it up for Julie and Emily to see.

Julie laid her hand on Millie's arm, to at least stop her from talking. "Millie, does your nephew know anything about flowers? This is Mrs. Dexheimer's daughter's wedding. It has to be perfect, as you can imagine." You have no idea, Millie, Julie said to herself.

"Oh, Luke's a natural. He and his partner were running an adorable flower shop up in Burlington, Vermont, but they broke up." She shrugged her shoulders. "He don't want to stay up there by himself, so he's selling the business and his house and moving down here. I figured it was time for me to retire anyway, what with seven little grandkids now. Hey, how's Tommy these days, Julie? I heard he packed it up and moved west."

Julie noticed Emily had wandered to the back of the store. She pulled Millie close and whispered, "Millie. She's loaded, and I need this wedding to be ideal. By the way, Tommy's fine." She made a mental note to call him.

Millie gave her an exaggerated wink. "Sure thing, doll." She led Julie, who still held Millie's sleeve, and walked toward Emily. "Miz Dexheimer? Let's talk about what would make your daughter's wedding the prettiest event it can be."

***

Finally she made contact with Thomas. "Tommy, what's going on? Last I heard from you, Maria's mother had a stroke." She carefully avoided any mention of the wedding plans, but didn't need to, as Thomas relayed the dreadful news.

"Jules, her mom wasn't going to make it. There were lots of complications, and anyway, we decided to get married in the hospital room. Everyone crowded in, the priest was there, but it was important to Maria. And the next morning, her mom passed away. We had the funeral service, and we're heading back to Phoenix tomorrow. She's just devastated."

"Oh." The word escaped Julie's lips like air from a slowly-deflated balloon. "I'm so, so sorry."

"Thanks, sis. Everyone took it hard, you know, such a big family, and she was the heart of it all. Maria doesn't even want to leave, but we have to go back." He cleared his throat. "Um, Jules, we're not going to be able to come up. Any time we have off, we'll probably fly to El Paso. Her dad, he's…"

"I know. Of course," Julie stammered. What could she say? "Listen, give Maria our love, and we'll talk soon. Love you, Tommy. And – congratulations on your wedding."

"Love you too, Jules," he said before disconnecting.

***

They had a baby shower in the barn in late August. It was a tiny event, and paid next to nothing, but Julie hoped it would drum up business. There was a fiftieth wedding anniversary party in September, the weekend that Thomas and Maria had set for their wedding reception. Thomas hadn't called since Maria's mother had died, but sent emails and a photograph of Maria in a simple white dress, standing next to her mother's hospital bed, her eyes shiny with tears. I'm sure that wasn't how she'd imagined her wedding day would be, Julie said to herself.

She'd have loved to travel out west, see her brothers, her sister, express her condolences to Maria in person instead of through a store-bought sympathy card and an Edible Arrangement. And to acknowledge their wedding, she wrote a generous check from her ever-dwindling personal account.

On the first day of autumn, Freddy cried. She'd never seen him cry before, not even that time he had what he described as 'a crab bisque that would make you weep' at Legal Seafoods. He slumped at the kitchen table after muttering something about a fuse box and the inspector.

"What? I didn't get any of that, Freddy."

He raised his head and blew out a sharp breath. "We didn't pass final inspection," he said. "The fuse box. I should have checked ahead of time, but we need special breakers for all the lighting. Oh, and the honeymoon suite's bathroom mirror is mounted too high," he added. "Unbelievable."

"Okay, no problem. Let's get that fixed."

He shook his head. "I can lower the mirror. But it'll be at least a week to swap out the fuse boxes, maybe ten days." He looked at Julie, who was scratching her neck. "Stop doing that, you'll bleed."

She looked at him quizzically, then realized what she was doing and drew her hand away, checking her fingers for traces of red. "Why does it take so long?"

"It just does," he snapped, and scraped his chair on the floor as he stood. "I'll get on it right away."

"We'll be fine," she called after him as he shut the door behind him. Right? *Right??* Even if it took two weeks, they still had four to go before the Dexheimer wedding. They'd be fine. She whispered those three words to herself all throughout the morning.

The Dexheimer wedding was going to be splendid. As the days grew shorter and the mornings were tinged with autumn chill, Julie worked hard. The few events they'd booked in the past two months had given them a tiny bit of cash. Mary Jo Browning came to lunch and promptly booked her parents' anniversary party in the barn. The wedding, though, would be their crowning achievement, and, fingers crossed, would lead to more. Freddy's friend Alison promised a mention in the society page's write-up of the wedding, and Freddy had chatted up the photographer. There would be plenty of shots of the barn.

Zack worked the grounds as summer flowed into autumn. His carefully-tended mums bloomed with hues of orange, bronze, and yellow. Pumpkins and gourds complemented the arrangements that surrounded the barn. He planted decorative purple cabbage in spots and was meticulous in his maintenance of the grass in the field between the barn and his cottage. A mild October with little rain kept everything in bloom.

Sarah perfected her cupcakes, and even tested a dark chocolate mousse cake on Freddy and Julie, who said it was perfect. She assisted in the kitchen, too, and seemed happier than ever that her vegetarian suggestions won over the head chef.

It was a Monday morning, about three weeks from the wedding, when Freddy burst into her bedroom.

"Jules! Wake up, come on!" He shook her shoulder, but she pulled a blanket over her head and grunted at him.

"Did you just say 'buck off'? I'm serious. Get up now." He pulled the covers off her and pulled her up to a sitting position.

"What the hell, Freddy? I don't have to be up yet."

"Oh yes, you do." He found her remote and switched on the small television, then flipped the channel to CNN.

Julie's sleep-encrusted eyes focused and widened as the details of the headline story sank in. Federal agents had raided and arrested eight men in a bust in Brighton Beach. She had never seen Viktor Polzin, but somehow she knew. He was one of those eight. She watched the footage of federal law enforcement personnel walking the suspects out of a squat building and wondered which one was Viktor.

"There, the young one. With the round face. I bet that's him," she groaned, pointing. Freddy sat on the bed next to her, his shoulder against hers. Neither of them spoke.

The house phone rang thirty minutes later. Julie answered and listened to Emily's weary voice.

"It's a nightmare. All of them were part of Viktor's uncle's business. They've been charged with defrauding Medicare of over a hundred million dollars. Margot refuses to believe that Viktor's a part of it."

"Emily, I'm so sorry." Julie accepted a cup of coffee from Freddy, who seated himself next to her at the kitchen table. She closed her eyes and waited, knowing what was coming next.

"He's a stupid boy, so she may be right, but it doesn't matter whether he knew or not. It's over."

Sure is, Julie thought. You have no idea.

"You've been nothing but professional and kind to us these past few months. It was a pleasure to work with you and Fred." At his name, Julie looked over to her best friend, who just shook his head. She felt her eyes fill with tears.

There were no words. Julie opened her mouth, and nothing came out.

"Thank you again, dear," Emily said before disconnecting.

Julie set the phone on the table. "That's it," she said. "We hinged it all on this wedding." She rubbed her eyes.

"Normally I'd say something funny, something to make you smile, but I'm depleted," Freddy said.

"I'll have to call the bakery, the florist. The band." She pushed her mug of coffee to the side. "Why did I ever think I could do this?" she asked to the ceiling.

"I need some air. Do you want to take a walk with me, Jules? Clear your head?"

Julie shook her head. "Nope. Going back to bed." She stood and scuffed out of the kitchen.

***

Two hours later, she was woken, again by Freddy shaking her shoulder.

"Jules, wake up! Come on!"

She threw back the quilt and glared at him. "More news on CNN? Not interested."

"Not that," he said, sitting on the edge of her bed. "While you were sleeping, I took a call from someone interested in booking a wedding here."

"Yeah, right. A wedding that'll be cancelled. Bad luck comes in threes, you know."

"Stop it. I've got the information. She's hoping for the holiday week." He pulled a scrap of paper from his back pocket. "A hundred people at the most. Simple, civil ceremony." He squinted at the paper.

"You need reading glasses, you know," Julie said. "Something chic."

Freddy crossed his eyes at her.

"Okay? Look, it's our first year. These things happen." He leaned in close to her and cupped her chin.

"We lost the Dexheimers, let's book this one. And whatever else we can."

Julie nodded, and bumped her forehead against his in solidarity. "Let's do it. But do you mind calling her back and working with her, at least in the beginning? I just can't find enough chirpy happiness to put in my voice right now."

***

While Freddy coordinated details with the new bride-to-be, Julie dealt with cancellations for the Dexheimer wedding. She was able to contact the bakery and the band, but there was no answer at Millie McNiff's flower shop, and no answering machine. Wasn't Millie's nephew taking over? She'd have to go there in person.

There was a brightly-colored flag flying outside the shop, and an 'open' sign on the door. A bell tinkled as Julie stepped inside.

"Hello?" she called.

"Be right with you!" a male voice replied.

As she waited, Julie breathed in the scent of sweet pea, gardenia, and roses. There was an arrangement on the counter in shades of yellow and peach.

"Hi, how can I help you?" He stepped out from the back room and extended his hand. "I'm Luke."

He was cuter than the photograph, Julie thought. She took his hand. "I'm Julie Tate. Are you going to keep it Millie's Flower Cottage?"

"No," he chuckled. "I love my aunt, but this place is now called Flowers by Luke. I'm just waiting for the new sign to be delivered," he added, with a glance to the front window. "You knew my Aunt Millie? She retired last week."

"I know, she told me she was going to, and that the business would be taken over by you. I have flowers ordered for a wedding on the fifth."

"Oh yes! The Dexheimer wedding. I have everything here in the computer. What time should we deliver, Julie?"

"Well, there's been a change. Actually, the groom was arrested and the wedding's off."

"Oh, no," Luke said, typing something into his computer. "What a shame." He looked up. "These things happen. You know, arrests," he deadpanned.

Julie's jaw dropped until she realized he was kidding. "Well, we're hoping to have another, different wedding over the holidays, and I'll definitely steer any business your way."

"Sure, just do a background check on the bride and groom first," he said, his eyes fixed on the computer monitor. Julie stared at him until he looked up. "Kidding! Again!"

He was just like Freddy that way. Wait. An imaginary light bulb went off in Julie's head. Hadn't Millie said Luke had just ended a relationship? He was cute, from the photograph that Millie had shown her. She'd surprise Freddy. "Luke, you're new in town. Would you come to our house for dinner? Say, this coming Friday? My business partner Freddy and I would love to get to know you."

Luke smiled at her. He looked like a matinee idol. "Sure, that would be great. I close the shop at five on Fridays."

"Fabulous! Come any time after that. Looking forward to it." Julie shook his hand again and marveled at the softness.

***

Just as Julie was pulling into the driveway, Freddy was backing out. She shifted into park and exited her car, stopping at his driver-side window.

"Where you headed? I have some news."

"I need to go to the bank," he said. "You know, armed robbery."

"Terrific. Get a lot of money. Will you pick up some coffee? Oh, and we're having a dinner guest on Friday – the guy who took over Millie's Flower Cottage. His name is Luke," she said, wiggling her eyebrows. "And he's very cute. I think he's perfect for you."

Freddy rolled his eyes. "You could have at least let me meet him and determine that for myself first. Fine," he added when he looked at her face. "I'll pick up coffee." He pulled away with a wave of his hand, and Julie called after him, "And money!"

FREDDY

Freddy drove into the weed-sprouted parking lot of Sarkis Jewelers in Middlefield. He cut the engine but didn't get out of the truck. In his pocket, he had his mother's platinum wedding band, her two-carat diamond engagement ring, and three other pieces of weighty gold. He steepled his hands in silent prayer, took a deep, cleansing breath, and went inside.

Thirty minutes later, he drove to the Pittsfield Savings Bank and strode into the lobby. His favorite teller Delia was on duty and she beamed when she saw him.

"Hey, handsome, how's everything?"

"Everything is the way it should be, I suppose, D. How are you this morning?" He handed over a deposit ticket and the check from Moses Sarkis.

"Hmm," she said, looking down at the check. She glanced up at Freddy with questioning eyes.

"No worries," Freddy said. "Some of my mother's jewelry that I've been meaning to sell for a long time. It'll help us pay a few bills, until we're raking it in." He craned his neck to look to the far corner of the bank, where LeeAnn, the branch manager, had her office. Instead of LeeAnn, he saw a man sitting at her desk.

"Hey, where's my girl LeeAnn and who hijacked her office?"

Delia made a face. "They transferred her. She's in Stockbridge now. But Bob's nice."

"Man, I didn't even get to say goodbye." Freddy looked again. The manager had someone in his office.

"She got promoted. Bob started last Monday. He's super nice." She handed Freddy his deposit receipt.

Freddy glanced behind him and saw there was no one waiting in line. "So this guy Bob, is he single? Um, I'm asking for a friend." If Julie was bringing this guy Luke to try and fix him up, he should at least have someone there for her. "Wait, is he married?" Maybe Julie would like him, though, he thought. A banker. Steady, reliable. Maybe not a complete loser.

Delia smiled so wide it looked like her face might split open. "No, Bob's not married, Freddy," she said, batting her lashes.

His phone buzzed in his pocket. It was a text from Julie that said simply "Get home NOW."

"Listen, D, I gotta run, but tell Bob I'll call him, okay?" Freddy turned to leave, then stopped and blew a kiss to his favorite teller.

JULIE

When Freddy stepped into the kitchen, he saw Julie with her hands on her head, as if she needed to hold her brains inside, to keep them from exploding out of her skull.

"Doll! Where's the fire? Wait, tell me there's no fire, please?"

"The Christmas wedding, Fred. Do you know who you were talking to?" She lowered her hands and used them to grab his shirt. Gently, Freddy extricated her grip from the fine cotton of his classic fit mini gingham.

"Yes, Julie. Yes, I do. Her name is Candace and her fiancé's name is Orlando. The wedding will be held, in the barn's chapel, on December…"

"Candace! Candace Russell!" she practically spit out the name. "Ring any bells yet?"

"Babe, what is going on? You're like a wild woman."

Julie inhaled deeply and let the breath out through clenched teeth. "Candace Russell is the woman who took my job at PCM. I loathe her." She looked at Freddy's hands. "Where's the coffee?"

He sighed. "I forgot the coffee, Jules. Sorry. So, wait. You don't like Candace. This is a business arrangement, not the senior prom. She's going to *pay us*. In fact, she has already paid us a non-refundable deposit of twenty-five hundred dollars. So I think you could set aside your hatred for this woman long enough to plan her wedding."

Julie crossed her arms. "I'm sorry," she muttered, her gaze focused on the floor.

When Freddy stayed silent, Julie looked up and let her arms drop to her sides. "I am," she said. "I just couldn't believe it was Candy. She called, and it took me by surprise."

"Were you civil to her?" Freddy asked.

"Yes."

"Good. Because Candace Russell is our only hope right now, Julie. Your nemesis may very well save our behinds. And I need you on board with this event as much as you were with the Dexheimer wedding."

"I'm really sorry," she whispered.

"Of course you are," Freddy said, pulling her to him. "Because you're a nice person. Otherwise I wouldn't be best friends with you." He kissed the top of her head.

FREDDY

Freddy called Delia and caught her just before the bank closed.

"Everything okay, sweetie? You ran out in such a hurry earlier," she said.

"Yeah, all is well, D. Listen, can you connect me with Bob, the new guy? Unless he's left already."

She giggled like a teenager. "Hold on, I'll put you through."

His voice was strong and clear. "Bob Vincent here."

Freddy coughed. "Hi. Um, Bob. I'm Fred Campion, over at Jingle Valley. I stopped in today, but you weren't available. Hope I didn't catch you at a bad time."

"Not at all. What can I help you with?"

"Well…" Freddy paused. This would have worked so much better in person. "Well, actually, Delia said you were new in town, and my business partner and I are hosting a small dinner party on Friday evening. Kind of a welcome-to-Dalton thing. I really meant to introduce myself today, but you had a customer…" Oh, man, he was babbling. He never babbled.

"That sounds great. And thank you. Being new in a small town does pose some challenges. Friday is fine."

They confirmed times and directions and Freddy hung up, satisfied that at least he could offer someone to Julie, especially as she was playing matchmaker with Luke. So that was four of them. Should he include Zack and Sarah? If they came, he'd have to do a complicated menu, and Sarah, well, Sarah was odd, let's just say it. He'd leave that for another time.

He called Candace Russell and got her voice mail.

"Candace, hi, it's Fred Campion at Jingle Valley. Calling to see if next weekend would work for you. You're going to love it here, and it'll look fabulous with all the holiday decorations in place. Let me know as soon as you can. Looking forward to seeing you." He ended the call. Candace was probably shocked to discover Julie was co-owner of the place, unless her old pal Harmony had sent Candace their way. Freddy smiled. That was probably it. Anyway, he'd deal with the bride on all business matters. They really needed this event. How much animosity was there between them, anyway? Candace had given them a deposit, and he could probably lock Julie away until New Year's.

***

"You know, I can get out of your way Friday night," Julie said, folding clean clothes and making piles on the dining room table. "I mean, I'll stay for dinner, but if things are going well with Luke, I can fake illness or something and go to my room. Should we include Zack and Sarah? For reinforcements?" She placed the square and rectangular piles back in the laundry basket, a devilish grin on her face.

"Oh! Well, here's the thing. I invited someone for *you*," he pointed to her. "There will be four of us, and I think we'll leave Zack and Sarah out of this one."

Julie narrowed her eyes. "Who did you invite?"

"The new manager at the bank," he said. "Bob! He's cute. And he's a Bob!" Freddy displayed jazz hands as he said Bob's name.

"What happened to LeeAnn? And did you do this to get back at me for Luke?" She fisted her hands on her hips.

Freddy chuckled. "Not at all! I really think you'll like him, and it wouldn't be fair to just have Luke. Honey, when I date, you date. That's the deal." He took her fists and uncurled the fingers. "Say thank you," he whispered, inches from her face.

"I'll hold my thank you until after I meet this Bob," she countered. She let out a heavy sigh. "I'm tired of dating. Even though I haven't had a date in months, still. What should I make for dinner?"

Freddy stepped back and wrinkled his forehead in thought. "We don't know either of them, so best to go with something safe."

"Chicken," they said in unison.

JULIE

Julie chose one of her "city" dresses in dark green. It wasn't over the top fancy, she rationalized, but soft and feminine. After all, she couldn't meet this guy Bob wearing her usual jeans and sweatshirt.

"Should I wear dark green, too?" Freddy asked, standing in her doorway. "Julie, sweetheart, you're perfect."

"Not too overdone?" She twisted her neck to inspect her backside in the mirror over her dresser. "I don't want to look desperate. I don't want to *be* desperate! God, this is why I hate dating." She turned her face to him. "And no, you should not wear the same color! We're not a couple," she reminded him. "But you are my best friend. I don't know how I would have gotten through these past few months without you, Freddy."

"Right back at you, sister golden hair," he said, glancing at her bare feet. "Wear flats. I don't know how tall he is."

Julie rolled her eyes. "What?"

"Casual shoes, dear," he said, wiggling his chin. "Okay, I'm just heading up to put on a clean shirt. My blue shirt. You need anything done in the kitchen before I go upstairs?"

Julie shook her head. "Everything is all set. Freddy," she called to his retreating back. He turned to her expectantly. "I hope it works out, for one of us, at least."

In three long strides he was standing in front of her.

"Let's just treat it as a casual meal with a couple of new guys in town," he murmured. "No expectations, okay?"

"Okay," she said.

***

Luke arrived first, and Julie invited him inside while Freddy was still upstairs. He was so handsome, like a swarthy Kennedy, all thick hair and white teeth.

"Luke, hi! So glad you could make it," she said. "Come on inside," she said, leading the way through the kitchen and into the living room. "Fred should be down any minute." She reminded herself to call Freddy Fred in front of Luke.

"These are for you," he said, offering a bouquet of lavender and orange roses. "Lavender for enchantment, orange for fascination. You are stunning in that dress."

Julie paused, and looked at Luke, whose dark eyes held hers. "Uh, thank you! They're beautiful." She glanced away, wondering what could be keeping Freddy. "Would you like a drink? I have wine, or a beer if you want. It's right in the kitchen," she stammered, feeling the heat on her cheeks.

"Nothing right now. I'm happy right here."

Well, isn't he the charmer, Julie thought. Just like Freddy.

FREDDY

Freddy descended the stairs as quietly as he could and caught sight of Luke. Julie wasn't wrong, he was good-looking, but Freddy was perceptive and could read body language. And what he was reading was not the movement of a gay man. Nope, old Luke had it hot for old Julie.

"Well, that's just great," he muttered, stomping on the last four stairs as there was a knock on the door.

"Freddy! There you are! Come say hello to Luke while I get the door." Julie practically ran into the kitchen as Freddy approached Luke with his hand held out.

"How you doin'," Freddy said, with the look of a man who's been beaten at his own game. "Glad you could make it." He'd enjoy himself, at least, watching Julie choose between her two suitors.

"Here's Bob!" Julie said, entering the room with Bob. "So, Fred, you two've already met. Bob, this is Luke Plante."

Bob reached for Luke's hand and shook it, then turned to Freddy. "Actually, Fred and I haven't formally met," he said, taking Freddy's outstretched hand and holding it in his.

Whoa, hold on a minute, thought Freddy. Bob? Julie's Bob??

"Bob." Freddy's head tilted a fraction as he held Bob's hand.

"Fred."

Their hands were still joined. Bob released his first, then blushed. Freddy found that adorable.

"Huh," Freddy said, unintentionally. Recovering, he added, "I'm so glad you could make it. Wow, I didn't have a chance to meet you at the bank."

Bob was tall, like Freddy. Lean, boyish. High forehead and straight nose. Pale blue eyes. And impeccably dressed in navy trousers and a clean white shirt open at the neck.

"Thanks for inviting me," Bob said.

"Should I open a bottle of wine?" Julie chirped.

"Let me help you," Luke said, taking her elbow.

Julie considered Bob, then Freddy. Then Luke. Freddy looked like he was lit from within. Positively glowing.

"Huh," she said, unintentionally, then let Luke escort her out of the room.

JULIE AND FREDDY

Mrs. Dexheimer's check arrived via FedEx the following week. Her handwritten note was enclosed. Dear Julie and Fred, Morton and I want to pay you for your work. Even though there won't be a wedding, you both spent hours of time planning it for my daughter, and you should be compensated.

Julie held the notecard in her hand, weighing the heavy paper stock. The envelope was lined with aqua tissue, and Mrs. Dexheimer wrote in that girls' boarding school backward slant. She set it down and opened the other envelope.

"Wow," she whispered, looking at the cashier's check. "That's a lot of money." Emily and Morton Dexheimer compensated them eighty per cent of the total cost of the wedding.

"FREDDY!!" Julie yelled. "Come quick!"

He clattered down the stairs and rushed into the kitchen. "What? What happened?"

Julie handed him the check and grinned.

"Holy shit," he breathed. He sat down hard and continued to stare.

"I know! I can't believe it," Julie said.

Freddy set the check on the table as if it might explode. "I'll take this to the bank today."

"Of course you will," Julie said with a knowing smirk. "And because it's such a big check, I think the manager should handle this one."

He smiled back. "Coupla matchmakers, that's us." As she stood, Freddy reached out for her hand. "Sit for a second. I need to tell you something."

"Oh no. No, Freddy. Oh, and with the sad-dog eyes?" She slumped back into her chair. "What?"

"It's not that bad, really. But I invited Candace Russell up this weekend. She needs to make a tour of the place. I'll do the whole thing if you'd rather not see her. You can hide out in your bedroom if you want. Or, stay at Luke's." He raised his eyebrows.

Julie laughed and sat up straight. "You know what? I'm looking forward to seeing her. And meeting the guy who wants to marry her! Really." She laid her hand over Freddy's, hers small in contrast to his. "I'll be fine. I'll even be welcoming and gracious. Let's take them out to dinner," she added, holding up the check.

"All six of us?"

"All six of us," she said. "Candace Russell's wedding will be the highlight of the year."

"It's on December 31, Jules."

"Still."

THE END

ACKNOWLEDGMENTS

As always, I offer my love and thanks to my husband, Jim. He is my biggest supporter, and everything I'm able to do is because of him.

I'd like to thank my author and writer pals, each of whom contributed to this effort and gave me feedback, advice, encouragement, and vital information: Brea Brown, Darcie Czajkowski, Elizabeth Marx, Meredith Schorr, and Pauline Wiles. Read their books – they're funny, intelligent women who know how to tell stories!

Also to my friend Celia Staperfene, who helped me understand more about Phoenix, Arizona and the surrounding area.

Kind thanks to Richard Haupt, Building Inspector for the town of Dalton, Massachusetts, who helped me answer a few technical questions, and who informed me, after this manuscript was written, that weddings in Dalton are crushed in the permitting by neighbors who don't want the noise. Well, that's why it's called fiction!

This beautiful cover is thanks to Carol Wise of Wise Element and author Heather McCoubrey (read her books, too!).

And finally, it's you, the reader, who enables me to continue this passion. Know that I am very grateful for you and for your love of reading.

Made in the USA
Middletown, DE
08 November 2015